WILD ABOUT RORY

SARA BLACKARD

Inked Heart Press, LLC

*For my weekly Zoom reader groups.
Thanks for being a high point in every week. Our chats have kept
me sane and encouraged me more than I can ever express.*

Chapter One

-Rory-

The temptation to pick up my computer and chuck it against the wall shakes my hands so violently I sit back in my chair and tuck them beneath my armpits. I scan my words filling the screen again. Crashing into the wall and breaking into pieces won't be nearly good enough for the manuscript.

Not by a long shot.

What it really needs is to be shoved so far into the trash can—the one at the back of the kennel used for dog poo—that feces will ooze beneath all the keys and fill up all the plug-in jacks. The satisfaction that washes over me as I picture snapping on the latex gloves and pushing my mutinous device deep into the smelly can lifts a gleeful smile on my lips that I'm sure would scare people.

Fitting, since the words typed across the page are utter crap.

Too bad the words are mine.

I roll my chair back from the desk and stand so fast

the chair slams into the filing cabinet behind me with a loud *clong*. I've written over thirty books, a good chunk of them hitting the *USA Today* bestseller list. Shoot, I've even had a couple go all the way to the *New York Times* list, so I know I can write.

This book—this idiotic, banal, stupid book (and, yes, I know idiotic and stupid are basically the same thing, but—GAH!)—has transformed from one I thought would hit it out of the park to the bane of my existence. It's not just imposter syndrome talking here. This book's such a hot mess even the dogs out back would take one look at it and lift their legs.

My problem?

I'm out.

It's like all my addicting adventures and exciting words have dried up. And I'm not just talking we-need-some-rain parched. I have full-blown, wildfire-has-come-through-and-incinerated-everything brain function.

It's a problem.

No.

Disaster of worldwide proportions, more like.

I've already pushed back my deadline with my editor and moved my release date once. If I can't figure out where the heck my evasive muse ran off to, I'll have to cancel my pre-order and lose thousands of orders. My readers will revolt, swearing off my books forever. I'll become an even lonelier loser with only my pathetic dog and glory days of minuscule fame to keep me company.

I glance down at Chub, my lazy as all get-out English bulldog. "No offense, buddy."

He lifts his droopy eyes to me—because lifting his head would take too much effort—cocks one eyebrow in question, then rolls to his side with a tired groan and falls back to sleep.

Yep.

I'm pretty much doomed.

My phone dings my tone for Jodi, my writing critique partner, just as panic laces my lungs shut. I snatch my phone like it's the only thing that can save me. Not that she'll be able to help me anymore than she already has. I've spent the last two weeks bombarding her with so many frantic messages that even I want to block myself.

Jodi: Hey, Rory. I hate to ask this with everything you've got going on, but have you seen your latest review for *Washed Out* on Goodreads?

Me: Um …no. <worried emoji>

Jodi: I wouldn't fret too much, and I definitely wouldn't comment, but it's getting more attention than it should.

That panic I mentioned a few seconds ago? Yeah, now it's so tight, black spots block most of my phone screen. I pull up my Goodreads app and click on my book, quickly scrolling down to the reviews.

At the sight of the review, my knees give out right along with my lungs. I aim for the chair, miss it completely, and go sprawling next to Chub. He paws my hand, since it landed on his legs and he doesn't have to actually move. The lick on my cheek surprises. He did have to stretch a bit for that, like he knew I needed bolstered.

"You're right. It can't be that bad." I rub behind his ear and reach for my phone, which had landed in Chub's drool puddle next to his water dish.

I wipe off the wet mess, glad at least the phone hadn't landed all the way in the bowl, and open the app back up.

The review's bad.

So much worse than Jodi implied.

Fret?

Oh, no.

I'm on vomit-level freak out.

The reviewer, someone I've never even heard of, hasn't just left a one-star with a "This book sucked." Nope. This person's left a good 5,000-word-count monstrosity. She doesn't just bash the book but questions my ability to construct an entertaining sentence and my worth as a human being, inserting far too appropriate GIFs into the review. I didn't even know that was a thing!

I scroll further down.

It just keeps going.

And going.

Getting worse and worse.

Convincing myself it doesn't matter, since it's only Goodreads, isn't possible. Why would someone go through this much trouble over a book they didn't like? If the book's truly this bad, why not DNF it and be done?

I finally get to the bottom of the review, after giving my finger carpal tunnel from having to scroll for so long. The screen blurs, and my entire face tingles in that I'm-about-to-cry way. The review was posted yesterday, and there are already over a hundred comments.

One hundred and twenty-two to be exact.

Oh, wait.

Twenty-three.

I blink to clear the tears as I quickly skim the responses. A lot of readers have come to my defense. Way more are applauding the reviewer for her dissertation. And she's responding to them, like keeping the let's-destroy-Bristol-North's-writing-career-completely party going is her entire reason for living. Sure, it's a pen name, and I could start another. But this is just … brutal.

I know I shouldn't engage. Authors have made that mistake in the past and paid dearly with their life. Not literal life, but their writing life—poof—gone.

My eyes focus on the reviewer's latest comment. The words freeze my finger just above the reply icon.

This book's only good for one thing: the dumpster—preferably a smelly one.

My body slumps as my eyes snap to my computer. Wasn't I just thinking that exact same thing? Writing the last few books has been like panning for gold in an Alaskan river—tiring, tedious, with only teeny flecks of hope to keep me going.

That still doesn't excuse the nastiness spewing from this woman. It does, however, prove my point. I'm in serious trouble of losing the one thing in life that has brought me excitement.

Writing's how I feel alive.

How I experience life's risks.

I've never been without it.

Ever.

I scan my phone screen again. The hateful words burn in my gut. Gritting my teeth, I let out a challenging growl and chuck my phone across the room.

I don't get shattering glass and exploding-metal satisfaction, but I'd probably regret destroying my phone, if I did. Just the act of defiance invigorates me, though. The next few breaths fill my lungs with the heat of determination.

I refuse to be a "washed up" writer. (Why, oh why did I title the book that?)

Books are my life, my passion. Without writing, all I have are Chub, the cinnamon rolls from the local coffeeshop, and a handful of weekly hours doing the admin necessary to keep the kennel I own with my sister and cousins running.

I'll prove this horrible person wrong.

My gaze skips back to the drivel-filled computer screen, and I swallow down the doubt clogging my throat.

I just have to figure out how.

Chapter Two

-*Dax*-

Hands grab my thighs beneath my butt cheeks as I bend my knees. The hooker winks, attempting to confuse me, then chucks the ball from behind the touch-line of the rugby pitch. I jump, soaring into the air as the lifters straighten their arms and tighten their grip on my legs, pushing me higher. I stretch my inner hand up, reaching beyond the other team's lock.

The ball surges higher with the ill-attempted toss. I shift my arm, my fingers grazing the leather at the last second. I flick them back, sending the ball into my team member's waiting hands. The thrill of victory's short lived as my body rushes back to the ground where the other players battle for position on the pitch.

As I sprint toward the ball, I glance at the score-board. Only four minutes left of the game. The crunch of an impact and low grunt snap my eyes back to the ball. The controlled chaos of the breakdown pulls a grin on my lips. The scramble's tight, and the instant I realize the ruck won't be cleared, I holler at my teammates.

"Ruck up!"

The opposition's eyes widen in worry a second before I slam into him and bind over my teammate still curled on the ground protectively around the ball.

"Dang, Dax." Dave Cook, my opponent, grunts as he pushes against me. "Mind taking it easy? I've got a date tonight and want to be able to move."

I dig my feet into the ground and engage all my core and leg muscles as I drop as low as possible over the ball. The burn energizes me like a drug—one I'm completely and openly addicted to.

"Take it easy in practice, and you take it easy when it matters, Cook." I lean my head against his as the ruck pushes against me.

"Hey," my best friend, Tony, huffs out as he attaches to the side of the ruck, his feet working to connect with the ball. "Did you see that Shelly's here?"

"Too focused." I groan as another player adds his push against us. "Unlike you."

"I'm telling you. She's totally into me."

If Tony can talk, he's not working hard enough, and we'll never win the tournament this year.

"Tony."

"Well—" *Oomph.* "She's about to get an eye full of flawless masculine dynamism."

"Dina-what?" Cook half laughs, half gasps in my ear.

"He's been reading the thesaurus again." I can't believe we're chitchatting in play.

This conversation needs to end before we waste the rest of the practice talking about Tony's love life. I push with everything in me, tipping the scrum backwards and exposing the ball.

"Get ready for greatness," Tony says as he swipes up the ball and takes off infield.

I peel off of the other players and hurdle over the man still in the fetal position on the ground. Tony's in a dead sprint toward the try line. My eyes dart to the clock on the scoreboard. Thirty seconds left. He might actually make it and win the scrimmage.

I push to catch up as the rest of the players on the pitch rush toward the ball. Tony, in a display of pure cockiness, points the ball at Shelly as he passes where she's standing on the touchline.

Show off.

Out of nowhere, Pete, the smallest man on the pitch, plows into Tony. The onlookers gasp. Tony's arms fling upward, losing the ball. I can hear the crunch of the collision over the pounding blood in my ears. Tony bounces off the ground, his head snapping with the impact, and his legs flail wildly like a cartoon with the sudden stop.

The ball careens down field just as the referee's whistle blows, ending the game. I jog up to Tony and Pete, both groaning where they lay on the grass. Wiping the sweat off of my forehead onto my arm, I rest my hands on my knees and laugh.

"That was quite the display of dynamism." My lungs heave, and I suck in air like I'm starving. "From Pete. Tony, I'm not sure what to call your display."

"Me. Neither," Tony says through pained breaths.

"That hit was epic." I slap Pete's knees.

"That hit hurt like crap." Pete rolls onto his knees with a groan.

"Man, remind me to avoid you when we practice in

the future." Tony pushes Pete over, then clutches his side. "You're a beast."

"Good practice, boys." I stand and clap, drawing all my team's attention. "Next time, less chitchat. We're not here to chatter like a bunch of women at book club."

"You know all about that, right, Ink Drinker Dax?" Tony groans from the ground.

He's always razzing me about reading. Has called me that since high school, when his French teacher claimed that was what the French called a bookworm.

Not that I'd ever go to a book club.

One, I'm too busy with building my gym into the next nationwide phenomenon. And two, that would require me to be around people and actually small talk. I'm not a big fan of either.

"Right. At least I know how to read." I kick Tony in the backside as I walk off the field and yell, "Same time next week. Be prepared to run drills."

The team moans, but they'll put their all into it next week. We all do. Rugby gets in your blood and demands your respect. Anything less would be dishonoring to the sport, the team, and everyone who's played before us. It's why I still play competitively and also coach the next generation.

When I get to my bag, I snatch up my phone. Fifty-three texts and voicemails wait for me. The exhilaration and the peace—as backwards as that sounds—of being on the pitch evaporates in a whoosh. I want to shove my phone back in my bag and see who's up for another match. Even though I'd like to, I can't ignore my responsibilities. The success of Body In Motion Gyms begins and ends with me.

Tony limps up next to me. Shelly supports him

under one arm, while he gives me a told-you-so grin. He peeks at my phone, his eyebrows riding up his forehead before his head shakes.

"It's Saturday, man. Time to take the day off." He reaches for his bag, not letting go of Shelly.

"Can't. You know, there's this thing called responsibility. You should look that up next time you scan the thesaurus."

"There's also this thing called life. It's something you haven't had in ages. Maybe never." He knocks his bag into my side. "I'm serious, Dax. It's time you delegate and stop running your corner of the world like it'll slip through your fingers."

"Yeah. Sure. I'll get right on that." Delegating would just add even more stress to my already heavy load.

"Sure, you will." Tony scoffs. "Keep it up, buddy, and you're going to live a long, lonely life. Unlike yours truly, who knows how to balance work and fun. Right, Shelbs?"

"Yep. Balance is important." She smiles up at Tony.

I grunt a non-response as they walk away. That's a great philosophy when you're an employee. It's easy to clock out when your shift's done and leave work behind. But I just can't. My business, this amazing thing I've built from nothing, needs all of me.

More if I'm able.

Chapter Three

-Rory-

"Pick up. Pick up. Grr. Pick. Up."

Each ring of the phone in my ear's like the dong of a death knell signaling the impending demise of my writing career. No. I'm not being dramatic. Not with how the review on Goodreads is turning into a full-blown assassination.

Sure, my sales have gone up. I about fell out of my seat again when I checked this morning. Those increased numbers came with a hefty cost—a drop in review rating.

Okay. I may be overreacting. There seemed to be just as many reviews raving about how wonderful the book is. But *Washed Up*'s now officially a 3.8 starred book.

I've never had so many one-star reviews. And each one chips at my already diminishing confidence that I can actually write a book people will want to read. We're not talking slow glacial melt, either. I've got chunks of esteem calving off me into the ocean of abysmal writing.

"Hey, sweet cheeks." Emmy, my cousin and inspiration behind my kick-butt characters, answers out of breath.

"Oh, thank goodness. I need your help." I start pacing my office in my house, stepping over Chub sprawled in the middle of the floor.

"What's up?" She grunts at the end of her question, and someone yells at her. "I'm fine." She hollers back.

I pull the phone from my ear. "What are you doing?"

"Practicing rock climbing on the office wall."

She works as a product tester at this amazing outdoor company, Ascent Inc., located up by Mount Denali. Basically, she gets to play for pay. She loves it, and it's perfect for her penchant for getting bored easily.

"Just how high on the rock-climbing wall are you?" I'm afraid to ask.

"Oh, near the top." Her words strain.

Emmy's boss's voice comes through the speaker, and I strain to hear what he's yelling at her. "Emmy, are you nuts? Do you want to get fired or killed?"

"Why's Bradley so angry?" Maybe I should just hang up and let her finish her climb, but there might be something here I could use in my book.

"Well, I wanted to see if I could free climb to the top."

"Emmy!" That wall's at least a hundred feet tall. "I'm hanging up."

"No." She grunts. "Just give me a second."

My heart pounds hard against my ribs as I listen to her strain. Any second she's going to drop, and I'm going to have to listen to her die. She huffs, then hisses. I can practically feel her struggle through the phone. I'm getting lightheaded just listening to her.

I roll my eyes and lean against my desk so I can look out my window to my safe perennial garden that holds all the thrills I normally get. Why did I have to end up with the wimp card in our family? My sister and all my cousins don't seem to have any qualms with finding excitement and adventure. They thrive on it. Where I'd rather write about it. Live vicariously through the characters I create with my lazy dog and pretty flowers.

"Okay." She huffs out a breath, drawing me back from the pity boat. "I can talk now."

"You're not hanging precariously from your fingertips?"

"Nope. I'm sprawled on the top landing, sucking air and ignoring my boss."

I picture the two-foot-wide edge at the top of the climbing wall at her work and shudder.

"He doesn't sound happy."

"He's threatening to fire me, but since he knows I'm the bomb diggity, he won't go through with it. Hold on a sec. Brad, I'll come down and grovel in a minute, okay? Give me a chance to catch my breath." She yells that last part in my ear, making me cringe. "Okay, Rore, what's up?"

"Well, I'm having issues with the book I'm writing—"

"Again?"

"Yeah, well—"

"At this rate, I should get a cut of your royalties."

"That's a little extreme. You're just giving me inspiration. It's not like you're writing the books." Though at this point, that might be a better option than me. "I'm just extra stuck this time. My head space is bad."

"Why?"

"Well … this reviewer basically roasted my last book on an important site. It's got over three hundred comments, most of them not good."

"*Washed Up?*"

"Yeah."

"I thought I performed especially well through your characters in that one." She chuckles, and I roll my eyes. "So, what's this reviewer saying that has you all frantic?"

"Oh, nothing much, just that my book lacks imagination, the writing could be done by a first grader, and, since the action feels completely contrived and banal, I probably haven't been out of the house I live in with my thirty cats for years." I blink the tears that blur my vision and slump.

"That's a bit harsh. You don't even own any cats."

I huff a laugh.

"Listen. You know I'm not much of a reader, but I love your books. And not just because you're my cousin. You've got talent."

She's the only one out of my family and friends that knows about my books. At first, I didn't want anyone to know, just in case I failed miserably. Then, later, it was nice having a secret, like the only thing I'd ever done that's rebellious. Now, I'm glad I haven't told anyone else, especially with how my writing career seems to be careening towards a cliff. Hearing that my non-reading cousin likes my books gives a little boost to my inner critic.

"Okay." I wish I could give her a hug.

"But …" Why does that one word carry so much weight? "Maybe she's right with some of it?"

And just like that, all my confidence shoots off the cliff into a free fall.

Emmy continues like she didn't just stab me in the chest with a dull pencil. "I mean, not much changes in your world."

"That's not true." I glance at the new artwork I just hung, but the defense falls short even to my own ears.

"Rory, come on. I know that I can stop in on any day and there will be Haagen Dazs Coffee Toffee Crunch ice cream bars in the fridge and that we'll take Chub to the end of the block and back around six. You order the same thing at the Rez every morning on your way to work, a medium peppermint mocha and a cinnamon roll, and, if I happen to come in on Thursday, I'll be joining you and Mark for a Bucket of Butt at Thorn's."

"Can I help it if they make the best fried halibut?"

"What you can help is changing things up. Find yourself an actual date. Go to the brewery, instead. Anything."

"I don't need different." I stomp around my desk.

"Yeah. I think you do. Your life's boring, and it seems like it's leaking into your writing."

Emmy has always been blunt. Not in a mean way, though today feels especially sharp. She'd just rather get to the point before she gets distracted. Normally, I love that about her. It seems freeing, as opposed to me always —*always*—thinking through every single word I say.

Today, it's a good thing I'm not talking to her in person.

I might be tempted to push her off the wall.

"My life being boring hasn't made a difference in the past."

"Well … it is now."

"Listen, I just need some advice on how to—"

"Nope." She pops the "p," and my mouth drops open.

"What?"

"I'm not helping anymore."

"Emmy." Panic makes me dizzy.

"Not until you get out of your comfort zone." Her firm voice doesn't waver.

My eyes dart around my office and out the window to my garden.

"What does that mean, exactly?" Because my brain stalled back on her "I'm not helping."

"That means you get out of your office—both of them. Do something, anything, to get some excitement churning." She laughs. "Who knows? You might find inspiration for your latest hero."

"So, if I change things up, you'll help me?" I'll push aside my discomfort for her help.

"I'll help you with technical questions, but adventures are on your own."

I slump into my chair. I've come to rely on her for ideas. I don't even know if I can come up with something by myself. What if I'm just a washed-up, has-been author with no real talent?

"Don't worry, Rore." Her voice has a confidence I wish I had. "I'm sure a change of pace will be exactly what you need to shake your brain loose."

"I hope you're right." I rub my fingers over my aching eyes.

"When have I ever steered you wrong?" She groans. "Now I have to go talk Brad out of firing me."

"Let me know how it goes." No, I'm not hoping karma bites her in the butt.

"You too." Does her chuckle sound diabolical?

I toss my phone onto the desk. Fine. I'll show her I can do change. Even if it's just to prove her wrong. At this point, I'm willing to try anything.

Chapter Four

-Rory-

I scan the bank of treadmills against the floor-to-ceiling windows at the local gym. They're spaced plenty far apart not to feel like the person next to me is breathing down my neck. The view of the bay's definitely better than my garden and will hopefully fulfill Emmy's declaration that I change things up. I've never liked the gym, so getting a membership's totally out of my comfort zone.

I'm surprised by all the open space in the building. The workout equipment flows spaciously in one area, leaving an open area on the other half. Except for the few people obviously here together, everyone seems to be doing their own thing and not paying attention to anyone else.

A lot of my anxiety of coming eases with that observation. No one will gawk at me. And if I come super early like I plan to, the chance of being ogled will be even less.

Not that anyone would ogle me.

My gaze snags on my reflection in the large mirror on the far wall. The bob cut of my strawberry blonde hair's as boring as my white capris and pastel, salmon-colored T-shirt. At least I show some pizazz with my turquoise glasses. I roll my eyes and turn toward the front counter. Ever since Emmy deemed my life dull, I'm seeing it everywhere.

But all that's about to change.

"I'd like to sign up, please." I force all hesitance out of my voice and smile confidently at the man behind the counter.

"Great." His enthusiasm as he goes through the membership benefits bolsters my spirits even more.

Ten minutes later, I open my car door with a sense of excitement rushing through my veins. Maybe Emmy's right? This could be just what I need. As I get ready to climb in and drive to the kennel, I spy a commercial fishing boat chugging out to sea.

"Chub, the office can wait."

I peek at Chub sleeping in the back seat. He doesn't even move. I chuckle, then snag my large peppermint mocha and cinnamon roll I had picked up on the way over from the passenger seat. I'm not even going to pretend it wasn't to comfort me after I braved signing up for the gym.

A girl can only change so much in one go.

I climb onto the hood of my car, prop my feet on the bumper, and take a long, soothing draw from the cup. Whoever put the gym here's a genius. Not only is there a killer view, but it's tucked away from the busyness of town. I can totally see wanting to take a hike along the coast after working out.

Well, that might be a stretch.

But I won't mind watching the boats, especially while enjoying a post-workout treat. I grab my cinnamon roll from the bag, inhale the sweet, spicy scent laced with yeasty goodness. Sinking my teeth through the crunchy outside to the gooey center might be one of the best parts of my day. I can't hold in the groan of bliss as the tasteful sugar hits my tongue.

"Well, if it isn't Aurora Wilde. Been a while since I've seen you." The voice that haunted me all through school sounds right next to me.

My eyes pop open, and my body jerks. I shriek, sucking in bits of cinnamon roll. Hot coffee spills down the front of me as my breakfast tries to kill me. I drop the pastry onto the bag and slide off my hood. Bits of bread and icing fly from my mouth. Even though the bite mocks me as a wet clump on the sidewalk, I can't stop coughing.

"Whoa, there." Dax Payton, my nemesis since third grade, grabs my coffee from my hand and sets it on the hood. "Just take a deep breath."

Easy for him to say. He's not choking on nothing. He puts his hand on my back between my shoulders. It's warm and stretches past both my shoulder blades, sending my skin crawling with a shiver.

I glare up at him, hoping an extra slobbery piece of roll will hit him square in the forehead. He steps back, and the same smug smirk he had growing up lifts the corner of his mouth. He reaches into his bag slung over his broad, very muscly shoulder and pulls out a water bottle. After he twists the cap off, he hands it to me.

Normally, I wouldn't take anything from the man. Actually, I probably would. I'm not big on confrontation. Normally, I would avoid him like I'm a baby seal and he's the devouring polar bear.

Avoid and evade has been my M.O. with this guy since I tried to be nice in third grade and give him my lunch when his stomach growled on the morning bus. He'd looked extra miserable that day with dark purple circles under his tired eyes and the way he'd hunched in on himself. We'd been assigned as partners on a history project and were going over the presentation one last time when his stomach rumbled so loud I felt it shake him. So, I'd offered my lunch like any normal person would. He'd blown up, said I was a pest, like a cat that wouldn't leave you alone, then twisted my nickname from Roar to Meow.

Since then ... enemies.

I snatch the water bottle from his hand and take a swig.

"Slow," he has the audacity to say.

I focus on the ocean, on my breath, on anything but the incredibly tall—and, admittedly, handsome—man hovering next to me. My throat spasms ease, but my face is an inferno. My blood has turned to lava and is displaying itself through my pasty, Alaskan skin.

"Better?" he asks, his voice all low and silky smooth.

My stomach flips. Maybe I'll get lucky and throw up on his tennis shoes. They look expensive, and puke's really hard to get out. Of course, my stomach calms, because when I want my body to revolt and spew on those deserving, it behaves.

Figures.

My sense of manners kicks in, and I nod an answer. Just because Dax Payton's a Neanderthal, doesn't mean I have to be. Just to prove so, I peek up at him.

"Thanks." See … totally civil.

"Sorry. Didn't mean to scare you."

He actually looks apologetic. Dax has never done contrite.

Ever.

Not in all those years he called me Meow. Not in the times he made fun of me reading at recess instead of playing. Not later in high school when he decided I didn't exist, even though we sat next to each other all junior year.

My body tenses, waiting for the verbal punch. There has to be some snide remark coming, and this time I'll be ready to spar. I've been honing my banter skills through each new book I release. I'm so ready for this. Except, no remark comes.

"That's okay." I feel my forehead wrinkling in confusion, so I smooth it into an emotionless mask.

"I haven't seen you here before." Dax crosses his arms over his chest, his biceps stretching the taut material.

Does the man purposely buy his shirts two sizes too small?

"Just signed up."

Though if I would've known he came here, I probably wouldn't have. Even if it's the only place in town to go, and I can't get my Emmy-spiration back without "changing my pace."

"Good." The corner of his mouth lifts again, like me coming to the gym's amusing, and he wipes the side of his lip with his finger and looks at my mouth.

Granted, I've never been big on exercise. I was that kid in school always missing the ball or tripping over my feet. The worst part? I shot up to five-foot-eight before my darn Norwegian genes ground to a halt, and everyone assumed with the rest of my family uber-athletic, I should be too.

"Be sure to take advantage of the two complimentary training sessions," he suggests as his gaze darts to my mouth again, like it's an automatic that I won't have a clue what to do.

It's true, but he doesn't have to point that out.

"Sure thing." I just need to stick to my normal Dax Payton approach and vanish.

I hope running into Dax won't be a repeat event. Most likely not, since I plan on being here extra early.

I shove my cinnamon roll in the bag and snatch my coffee. Both are going straight into the trash the second I get to the kennel. I squeeze between my car and Dax, trying not to make it obvious I'm avoiding brushing against him.

"Welp, gotta go." I force a smile, because, well … non-confrontational.

"Sure." He's chuckling and shaking his head.

Why's he chuckling?

I climb into my car, ignoring the fact that he's just standing there, staring. I wave, my nerves getting the best of me.

"See you around, Aurora." He tips his chin at me cockily and finally heads to the gym door.

His shoulders shake in amusement. I spear him in the back with eye daggers, hoping his skin's crawling from them. It's always that way with him.

Him picking at me.

Like why's he calling me Aurora? Why can't he call me Rory like everyone else? It's like that one act of kindness triggered his inner bully.

Well, I, for one, am past acting childish. I refuse to let him get a rise out of me anymore. Being the bigger person won't be hard, even with him standing over six-feet-five.

"Just keep to myself like always, right, Chub?" I tip the rearview mirror to see my dog's reaction.

There isn't one. What I do see is a blob of cream cheese icing stuck to my lip.

Great.

I bang my head on the steering wheel. Why can't I ever just play it cool when it comes to Dax? It's like my default setting's embarrassment, whether caused by him or myself. If this is what getting out of my comfort zone and finding my muse entails, I think I prefer letting my muse stay hidden.

Chapter Five

-Dax-

Fog hovers on the bay like an extra-hot sauna where you can't see to the other bench. A light drizzle streaks down the gym windows. The low thump of the *Call of Duty* video game soundtrack coming through the gym speakers counters the relaxing, early morning scene. A small, round black bear, unfazed by the rain, makes its way across the grass toward the barely visible shoreline.

Note to self: Let Tony know to remind the trainers to keep their heads on a swivel.

Usually, the bears steer clear of the facility during the day, when more people mill about, but bears don't always know what's best for them.

Kind of like people.

My arm shakes. The exertion of holding the side plank Vasisthasana pose threatens to zap my body of its strength. I maintain the position twenty more seconds, breathing through the pain and pushing myself even further. On an exhale, I move to plank, lower to the floor, and rest for thirty seconds. Then, I push up and repeat the pose on my other side.

Most people do yoga to relax. I call bologna. My modified yoga creates crazy strong muscles *and* flexibility. I can't get that with just lifting.

My hurdle to getting others on board with my program is most people who come to work out want straight-forward approaches, whether it's lifting, running on the treadmill, or Crossfit. Until I mixed up my own workout, taking bits and pieces of just about anything I could find, I'd stalled. As soon as I have the program perfected and can test it, I'm going to help others achieve their maximum potential.

The lock on the door clicks just before the door swings open. My eyes snap to the clock. No one ever comes at four forty-five. Shoot. The first people usually don't start trickling in until well after six.

My arm wobbles beneath me.

Focus, Payton. You do own a 24/7 gym.

I hate that I've let this interruption get in my head.

Faze me.

It just proves how off of my game I am.

I close my eyes and will everything to relax into the challenging side plank position. Each breath centers me. My hand pushes into the floor, supporting my wrist. The line from my wrist to my shoulder's sure and strong, like the Sitka spruce growing straight to the Alaskan sky. My core burns hot as my muscles hold me firm. Everything else disa—

"Oh." A soft gasp snaps my eyes open, and my gaze collides with none other than Aurora Wilde.

My elbow buckles. I barely catch myself and attempt to make the change in position look effortless. Breath heaving. Heart racing. You'd think I'd just ran the four-mile loop to town and back at a full sprint.

Why in the world is Rory Hates-Anything-Athletic Wilde here before most have even come out of REM sleep? Does it matter?

Yes, it most certainly does.

This is my time. My sanctuary before the storms of the day thunder down. Ever since I opened Bodies in Motion, my early morning workout with no one else around has kept me grounded. I've never had someone arrive before five-thirty, not once in the seven years since my grandma left me the money I needed to start up.

Of course, the one person throwing me off-kilter would be Rory.

I huff a silent laugh and push myself off the ground. Do I perform a super impressive handstand from lying flat on the ground before standing? Of course, I do. I need the reminder that I'm in control here. Nothing affects me.

Combats my focus.

Not even annoying interruptions.

I turn to face Rory. She's still standing on the opposite side of the half wall that separates the entry from the workout area. Her mouth hangs open as she stares at me.

Has she ever focused on me this long? Nope. Not since that day in third grade where she saw too much. Shoved me into a proverbial corner.

I take a deep breath and push the memory away. It's stuck, though. Her wide, blue eyes gaping at me as my nine-year-old self lashed out. I roll my shoulders with a huff, and Rory's mouth snaps shut.

Bright red blotches dot her cheeks, and I can't help

but smile. She fumbles as she pushes her glasses up and walks woodenly toward the treadmills. I nod in greeting. Her eyes widen, before she lifts her hand in a half wave from her side.

Cute.

That's what Rory Wilde is, from her chin-length hairstyle pinned back from her face she's had since we were fifteen years old to her purple tennis shoes that look like they haven't spent a day outside. Even her tank top with an otter reading a book's adorable.

Irritatingly so.

Everything about Rory has always been perfect, from her idyllic childhood to her doting parents. She always had straight A's. Was the teacher's pet, no matter what teacher it was. The only time a hair ever got out of place was during P.E. and she couldn't sweet talk the teacher out of participating. Between her sister and cousins, Rory may have gotten all the height, but she didn't get any of the athletic talent. It was the only black spot in her shiny, happy existence.

Seriously.

Flawless, perfect, and not to mention nosy. Aurora Wilde needed teasing to keep her humble.

At least, that's what I'd convinced myself during elementary school. It kept the focus off of me. Her focus, especially. She got really good at pretending I didn't exist.

Kind of like she's doing now.

I watch in the reflection of the windows as she sets her bag next to the furthest treadmill from me. She pops her earbuds in, then, after placing her phone in the holder, steps onto the machine. A few clicks produce a frustrated huff when the treadmill doesn't move. I should go help her, but a not-so-small, and—if I'm honest—petty part of me wants her to ask for help. It'd be a first.

She crosses her arms. Her mouth moves like she's talking to herself. I keep my amusement in and head to the pull-up bar where I can watch her without looking like I'm watching. This might be worth the interruption.

A couple more button pushes, and now her foot stomps.

"Stupid thing." Her muttering reaches me, and I bite the inside of my cheek to keep from laughing out loud.

I hang on the bar to stretch everything out from my floor exercises. She turns her head just a bit toward me. Her hand trembles as she pushes a stray hair out of her face. Guilt slides up my arms, making my fingers numb. My reasons for being a jerk in school don't dominate me anymore, so why am I acting petty now?

"Press the play button and choose your setting." I walk across the room.

"Why are there so many options? It's a treadmill. It should be a simple walk or run," Rory grumbles, still not looking at me.

"Well, Bodies in Motion promises top of the line equipment so its members can track as much or as little as they want."

It's been my philosophy from the beginning. Only offer the best and safest equipment, even if that means the business's expansion has to wait. Turned out to be the right choice, since it's one of the reasons for the explosive growth.

"Maybe walking trails would be better." She mumbles low, so I chose to ignore it.

See.

I don't have to slip into old habits and pick on her.

"Here. You just push the play button." I reach in front of her.

This close I can smell her, and it's like being back in high school. She always smells sweet, like she rolls in caramelized sugar before leaving the house. It distracts me now, just like it did back in class. Makes me want to lean in and savor it.

I don't.

Obviously.

For several reasons.

1. Aurora Wilde's attention brings nothing but trouble. I knew it clear as day back in 3rd grade.

2. She'd probably deck me in the face if I ever so much as hinted at just how distracting she is. I'd deserve it.

3. And most importantly, for me, Aurora Wilde equals confusion and nuisance. I can't afford either right now.

I'm attempting to make Bodies in Motion into something big. To prove to myself and others that I'm more than just a poor boy with no future. I've got investors practically panting to get in on the growth. One group, especially, could change my landscape forever. Letting my focus veer even a little off course now could ruin everything.

Which is why interacting with my personal siren, the one person who has beckoned me to confess all my pain and struggles since childhood, is a colossal mistake I can't afford to make. So, yeah, I may be a bit more gruff than necessary when I show her how the treadmill works. I might also cut my workout short to go for a run outside.

It gives me time to pull all the threads her presence unravels back into place. To retie the knots tight so they'll never come loose again.

When I was a kid, I used anger. As a teen, indifference worked best. Now, after years of self-discipline, I have the power to create my reality. And, in my new reality, Aurora Wilde isn't my doom. She's nothing but another client wanting to get in shape.

Chapter Six

-Rory-

How in the world can my shoulders hurt this much? And why on the one day that lifting my arm repeatedly is a given? I cringe as I stretch to put more paint on the mural I'm helping my sister Denali's boyfriend, Drew, create on the side of his animal rehabilitation center.

Well, my cousin Violet's the artist. The rest of us are just the grunts. I roll my shoulder, taking a step back to make sure I have my section right. Blues and greens mix to create a beautiful sky above the ocean and mountains filled with animals. It's coming along faster than I expected it to.

I scan the yard, my gaze bouncing off of all my family and my best friend, Mark. Drew's mom's still here from Australia, along with her fiancé, Vic. My eyes narrow on the couple as she points to tell him what to do and he just smiles at her. They got back together after years apart, their story inducing swoony sighs whenever they are around.

Maybe I need to shift away from romantic suspense

and write a less intense, second-chance romance? Or maybe I could put Vic and Stella in the outback with rabid kangaroos and blood-thirsty henchmen?

Ugh.

Lame!

I rub the back of my neck as I head to refill my paint. All the stupid gym has created is pained muscles. No inspiration. No muse racing back to help me.

I spy my cousin Sadie nudging her fiancé, Bjørn. He leans in, whispers something in her ear that makes her blush, then kisses her jaw. I roll my eyes and turn away only to find Drew flirting with Denali.

I'm surrounded by all this love blossoming. It should rejuvenate me, but all I feel is nauseous. I'm a romance author, for Pete's sake. My sister's and cousin's love lives should be filling me with ideas and excitement.

The tinge in my gut isn't happiness.

More like jealousy.

Depressing, I know.

I roll my neck and pour more blue into my paint cup. Letting their happiness get me down's not how I want my story to play out. People hit slumps. It happens. Sure, you'd actually have to have a love life for it to slump, but that's just a technicality.

"Are you hurt?" Violet steps up next to me and slides her hand across my shoulder.

"No. Just sore." I stir the paint with my brush, a little embarrassed to confess the next part. "I started working out at Bodies in Motion this week and did too much."

"We live in the most beautiful place in the world, and you workout inside?" Violet laughs, but it doesn't hold any judgement. "I love how you do you, no matter what."

"I'm indoorsy. What can I say?" I shrug, then cringe at the pain.

"You didn't used to be," Dad grumbles from where he's painting purple in the mountains. "Used to be we couldn't keep you inside. All four of you would run like wood nymphs through the forest, staying away for so many hours we'd start to worry. Remember that, hun?"

Mom nods. "Yeah. I used to want to chain you girls down, but your dad insisted being in nature was good for you."

"Heck, yeah. It was," Denali chimes in.

"Yeah." My response isn't as energetic.

I may say I'm indoorsy, but I actually love being outside. Love the wind teasing my hair and the way fresh, crisp mountain air invigorates me. I just prefer having clear barriers to protect me.

The outdoors is dangerous. I swallow the lump of fear in my throat as my eyes dart to Sadie's scarred arms. Not only will bears and moose kill you, but nature itself will flick its insidious fingers and destroy.

After Sadie and her friend Melinda had been crushed in that avalanche, intense trepidation overshadowed all desire to go outside. It still baffles me how the rest of my family wasn't fazed. I never wanted to live through the pain of loss and recovery Sadie did.

Why would I need to chance it when I could experience adventure through books? Loads of studies show that your brain doesn't distinguish between real excitement and fictional. So, by reading and writing, I give my brain more than enough stimulation.

Thank you very much.

No need to risk life and limb for a spruce-laced scent I can get from burning a candle.

As Violet joins Denali and Sadie in animated remembrance, I slink to my corner of the mural. They can relive our childhood all they want. I'd rather not have the grief that comes with it.

"I can't believe you're going to that gym," Mark hisses in my ear.

I jerk at his vehemence. "Why?"

"Dax Payton owns it." Mark drops the information then looks at me like I'm to blame.

Concerning? Yes, but I try to not to let this new information bother me.

Sure, I'm not thrilled with being a part of anything Dax has going on. But, despite being completely sore, I've actually enjoyed going to the gym every morning. Even with the Cur of Seward there most mornings with me. My lips tweak at the title.

I might need to lay off the regency romances for a bit.

"Well … it's not like I have many choices," I counter.

None. And avoiding interacting with Dax doesn't take any more effort now than it did back in school.

"How can you even consider giving him your money?" Mark's not letting this go.

"I'd like to think I've moved past high school, Mark. Besides, I like going. The facility's nice, and the views are stunning." Granted, most of the time I walk on the treadmill and type on my phone, but he doesn't need to know that.

Also doesn't need to know how I might peek at Dax in the windows' reflection while he's doing his insane workouts. Of course, I only peek for research purposes. He's definitely a cur, but he's a magnificently built one.

"I just don't want to see you hurt." Mark grabs my elbow and steps closer.

He's been my best friend for years and knows how much the teasing in school affected me. Ever since our parents started hanging out when we were in first grade, we've gotten along. Then, after Sadie's accident, we had even more in common since he wasn't much of an outdoor person, either.

"I'll be fine." I give him a smile, hoping he'll just drop the embarrassing conversation.

His thumb rubs along the inside of my elbow. I rotate my arm. I must have paint smeared there. Seems I've gotten blue everywhere.

Huh.

No paint.

I glance up at Mark. We aren't touchy-feely friends. I'm pretty sure he'd like it if we were, but we've been friends for so long, we're practically siblings. He drops his hand and picks up his cup of paint he'd set down. His ears and neck are as red as the salmon bellies he's painting.

"Oh, shoot," Kemp, Violet's best friend, says as he trips over the hose and fumbles with the brush and cup of paint in his hands.

"Again?" Bjørn calls out. "Man, you didn't take your anti-clumsy pills today or what?"

I love that Sadie's and Denali's boyfriends fit in so easily with our family. Kemp has been nervous all morning. He's given us enough fodder to tease him for months.

"Something like that." Kemp sets the cup and paint on the grass, his hands and shirt dripping bright pink, just as his phone rings in his pocket. "Great. It's my sponsor."

"Here. Let me help." My nephew, Sawyer, plucks Kemp's phone from his back pocket and hits the speaker button

"Hey, Martin. You leave yet?" Kemp's eyes dart to Violet, the nervousness from earlier ratcheting up even more.

"Just now. I wanted to call before we took off and let you know that the Nature Channel agreed to the switch in teammates," Martin answers.

What race? Kemp usually doesn't snowboard in the summer.

"Really?" Kemp pumps both fists in celebration, splattering purple paint everywhere, and throws Violet two thumbs up.

Everyone stares at Kemp as he talks to his sponsor. We aren't ashamed of listening. He's practically family since he moved up here for the summers and we adopted him into the fold. While Kemp's nerves have evaporated with the call, Violet looks like a snowshoe hare sensing danger. She keeps darting her eyes at the family and motioning for Kemp to hang up.

"Tell that fiancée of yours she's incredible. Anyone other than Violet, and I don't think the network would've gone for it. She's pretty amazing," Martin says, and a collective gasp waves through the family.

"Yep. Yep, she is." Kemp swallows and shifts on his feet, like he just now realizes he screwed up.

"The flight attendant's giving me the stink eye. I'll send you the information." Martin hangs up without saying goodbye, and an eerie quiet settles over our crowd.

We don't do quiet.

Ever.

"Explain." Uncle Will's face is stone hard as he looks between Violet and Kemp.

I lean forward a little in anticipation. Can you blame me? This is great research.

"Well, sir … it's, well …" Kemp stammers, and my smile stretches so far across my face, I can't even hide my glee.

"The Nature Channel's doing this extreme race through the Americas with different celebrity teams." Violet talks over Kemp. "Kemp's sponsor got Kemp in the race, which is amazing since the winners get to donate ten million dollars to the charity of their choice. Can you imagine how many kids Alley Oop could help in their winter snowboarding camps with that amount of money?"

I set down my cup of paint as I process what Violet just said. A race across the Americas would make an amazing setting for a book. Throw in foul play and some explosions, maybe a Central American drug cartel, and I'm sensing a bestseller.

"The engagement isn't even real, so don't worry." Kemp tries to ease Uncle Will's anger but fails miserably.

Too bad I don't write romantic comedies. A nervous giggle bubbles from my lips, and I press them tight together to keep the rest of my amusement in. The look on Uncle Will's face is priceless.

Violet rambles on about some woman snowboarder who practically stalked Kemp, but I'm zoning out as ideas start to spin. I won't be able to change my current mess of a manuscript with the race idea, but it could be my next book. I picture a faceless heroine rushing through the jungle as other competitors cheat in some horrible way, like pits with spikes or poisonous snakes in sleeping bags. It could work.

Kemp's attempting to explain why his sponsor thinks he's engaged to Violet, but from the look on Uncle Will's face, it's not working. Fake engagements aren't something that come up often in real life, though they sell like sourdough hotcakes in a tourist RV park in romance.

"Lots of people, if the books Rory writes are based on reality." My name coming from Sawyer's mouth pulls me fully back to the present.

Everyone's stare's now on me. Sawyer just keeps blabbing on about my books. How does he even know I'm an author? He's only eleven years old.

"Of course, there are all kinds of other situations in her books that seem farfetched but work out." Sawyer washes out his brush, not realizing he's imploding my entire secret world I've created for myself.

"What're you talking about?" Denali chuckles, bumping Sawyer's shoulder. "Rory hasn't written since high school, and definitely not books."

Obviously, I'm very good at keeping secrets.

"Sure, she has. She's written tons of books as Bristol North." Sawyer looks up now, those creases in his forehead getting deeper. "You guys didn't know that?"

If he wasn't so adorable and sweet, I'd kill him.

As everyone reacts, I'm shocked by their responses. Violet explodes with excitement. Apparently, my pen name, Bristol North, is her favorite author. My mom, the local college literature professor, is going on about how allowing me to read *Sweet Valley High* books led to my spiral into romance. Mark looks like I took every sick dog at his vet clinic and kicked them. Poor Sawyer has guilt tearing his eyes up like he's destroyed my entire world.

Keeping something this big from my family may have been a mistake.

I can't let Sawyer get upset about this. He's always been able to see what others don't, so it shouldn't be a surprise that he knew. I walk over to him as his eyes grow wider.

"Sorry." He cringes as his chin trembles. "It was just so obvious I thought everyone knew."

"It's okay." I pull him into a hug, letting his small arms around me comfort and ground me. "I guess I don't really need to keep it a secret anymore."

As Violet goes on and on about how amazing my books are it hits me. Keeping my talent, my passion, from those I love reeks of cowardice. When did I become so afraid of life—of being embarrassed or bruised—that I couldn't trust my own family? As I stare around at the people closest to me, their hurt slamming into my gut, I can't hide anymore. Like it or not, my covert attempts at embracing life from the sidelines are exposed.

And I'm not quite sure if the lightheadedness I'm experiencing is from relief or distress.

Chapter Seven

-*Rory*-

A light drizzle beads on my windshield as I stare out of it at the front door to Bodies in Motion. I'm not sure if I want to go in. I've thought a lot about what Mark said, and maybe he's right. As much as I like the change of pace, do I really want to give Dax Payton my hard-earned money?

He's been here all week, terrorizing me with his presence.

Okay … that's an exaggeration.

He hardly says hi. More grunts and nods his chin before ignoring me completely.

Which is part of the problem.

After lying in bed all night thinking about it, I see Mark's point. I've put myself right back in high school. Each morning, I come in and a small part of me hopes Dax will be human for once. Each morning with a grunt or barely a nod, he disappoints me like he did every day since third grade.

I don't want to do this anymore.

I have so much hurt and bitterness toward Dax, that Mark's right. I shouldn't give him my money. I shouldn't set myself up each morning for displeasure.

My eyes snag on the sign in the window beside the door. I can't read it from this distance, but the words are burned on my retinas.

Quitters Never Win.

No Refunds.

I groan, mad the stupid sign's right. Mad that the way Dax treats me still affects me. Thank you Enneagram and my dumb peacemaker penchant to want to please people, even the jerks.

Isn't that why I kept my successful author career a secret for so long? I knew Mom would be disappointed that I wasn't writing something more literary. Writing, especially romance, opened me up for so much flak, it's safer for no one to know who I was. I could just do my thing in the shadows of ambiguity and hide from the difficult.

It worked too.

At least until my ideas dried up, spiteful reviewers attacked, and my too-intuitive nephew outed me.

P!nk's song *Courage* cycles through my car's speakers, and I crank it up. I breathe in a deep breath and hold it, letting my fears and insecurities gather in my lungs like impurities. With a forceful huff, I push them out.

I'm done with being a coward. I'm proud of my writing and the business I've built. If the world knows who I am, who cares?

I'm also not going to let Dax's past bullying affect me anymore. I avoided him all through school, so I shouldn't have a problem pretending he's not here now.

Besides, he hasn't picked on me once all week. Hasn't hardly acknowledged me.

I'm pretty much not on his radar.

Which is exactly where I want to be.

P!nk's song gets to the chorus. I belt out the words, asking myself if I have the courage to change. I want to. I'm done being afraid—scared of what people think, of disappointing others, and rocking the boat.

I say a quick prayer for strength and turn the car off. Gathering my stuff, I keep singing the song to myself, allowing it to boost my courage even more. As I walk to the front door, my shoulders pull back. The early morning midnight sun peeks out from the clouds, and I lift my face to the rain-scented air and take one more fortifying hit before snapping the gym's door open.

The beat of the music Dax plays thrums through my blood, reinforcing my newfound boldness. I'm tempted to ask what the music is. I type faster here while on my phone with the energizing beats than I do at the office with my computer. But that would take talking to the man I'm determined doesn't exist.

My eyes scan the open area where the Cur usually works out. I scold them to behave and keep on the goal. As they skitter toward the treadmills, they skid to a stop on the most magnificent sight I've ever seen.

Dax uses one of the leg weight machines. Instead of sitting in the seat like a normal person, his legs thread through the brace backwards with his feet hooked under where a person's knees should be. His six foot-five-plus body sticks out like a plank a good three feet off the floor into the large walkway between the treadmills and the weight machines.

How do I know his height?

It was a bragging point of his during high school … before he stopped growing.

The big ox.

The abject man's not only shirtless but in shorts. Almost every single muscle on his body's engaged and showcased. These aren't your run-of-the-mill muscles, either. No, there are so many sections bulging across his chest, arms, and legs I never knew even existed.

My lungs and eyes burn, and I shake my head to jolt my senses back. I suck in a breath and flutter my eyelashes to dampen my dried-out eyes.

I can do this.

I can make my way to the treadmill without gawking. Besides, I don't *want* to gawk at the man and inflate his ego more than it already is. He's not worth my ogling.

Reminder firmly in place, I snake toward the treadmill I've designated mine. My dang traitorous eyes keep darting back to Dax.

Wait.

I'm going to have to pass just a few feet from him. There's no other way to the treadmills, even if I pick a different one.

I stumble and almost turn back. He probably did that on purpose. Exactly like how he'd lean over my desk in class, invading my space while simultaneously ignoring me, to talk to someone when he could've easily talked standing upright. I clench my teeth and stalk toward the treadmill. I'm not cowering anymore.

As I draw closer, I keep my gaze trained on the goal, which is a mighty feat when presented with a physique on display that I could easily use in a book. I pass with just a quick glance. His body trembles as he reaches for a large kettle ball set on the floor next to him.

"Morning," he grunts without actually looking at me.

"Yep," I squeak and pick up my pace while trying not to look like I'm running away.

Yep? I write books with thousands of words in them, and all I can choke out is "yep?" I take heart in knowing that most women, and men for that matter, probably couldn't help but stare at the display. This isn't a normal workout happening here. This is superhuman stuff.

Just sucks that Dax Payton's said superhuman.

Otherwise, I'd totally stare.

Mouth open, heart-racing ogling.

I make it to the treadmill without incident and plop my bag on the floor. I should probably put my bag in a locker in the changing room, but I'm avoiding the room like the plague. I'm not big on all the nakedness that happens in locker rooms. Just the thought of someone seeing me makes my face burn with embarrassment.

Once I pull up my notes app on my phone and start typing my next scene while I walk, I'm sure ignoring the overt showcase of ego will be easy. As I step onto the track and start pushing buttons, Dax lets out a low growl that flips my gut and sends shivers up my spine.

My head turns and mouth goes dry as Dax lifts the kettle ball by the handle with one hand toward the ceiling, perpendicular to his body, still planked parallel to the floor. When he gets to the top, he switches hands by heaving the heavy weight up slightly and catching it as it falls toward his body. As he lifts the next arm up, another growl reaches my ears.

I lean my forearm on the treadmill's display as my

knees go a little weak. It's demented that I should find Dax attractive in any way, but, at this moment, my imaginative brain's running through so many possibilities I can't help my increased heart rate.

Just how much can the man lift? What would those strong arms feel like wrapped around my body? Lifting tall, slightly fluffy me?

A beep sounds next to my elbow a second before the treadmill's track takes off at full speed. My feet shoot out from underneath me, crashing me to the track and sending me somersaulting off of the end. I land on my shoulders with my head looking between my tangled legs and arms and my bum in the air.

"Rory!"

Now he uses my name?

"Ow." A nervous giggle escapes, but even that hurts.

I try to roll over, but my feet somehow ended up pinned under the track. The spinning rubber yanks on the calves of my pants, inching them down. Oh, please Lord, please. I cannot end up with my pants around my ankles.

"Really?" Dax's muscled calf fills my vision a second before he hits the off button.

"Your idiotic machine has too many options." I groan, peeking up at him through my legs.

"Sure. That's what caused it." He smirks, and my face flames even hotter. "Are you hurt? Can you get up?"

"I don't know. My feet are stuck."

He bends down and whistles. "You really got it good, cupcake."

Cupcake?

What the heck is that? He hasn't talked to me in years, and he throws out a moniker like cupcake?

"Can you unpretzel yourself?" he asks gruffly, but his hand on my back is gentle.

When I try to roll my head to the side so I can lay flat on my stomach, a knife pain stabs into my ankle. I cut my yelp short with a groan. Squeezing my eyes shut, I will the tears away. I don't want to show weakness. That would just make this entire embarrassing situation worse.

"Okay, Wilde. Hold still," Dax practically growls at me.

Yeah, well, my workout just got ruined too. And it's all his big, hulking self's fault. I'll never admit that, because then he'll know how enthralled I was. And that's fuel I'll never give him.

"I'm going to lift the machine." He bends his head down to peer under the treadmill, his hand touching my ankle. "I'll have to lift it straight up, though. If I tip it, I'm afraid it will hurt your ankle."

His annoyed tone has me rolling my eyes. I want to snap back a snarky comeback. It's on the tip of my tongue, but I just can't push it past my lips. Then he steps one foot over my legs and all snark shrivels up.

I'm dying.

Cause of death?

Mortification.

Sure, we both have legs a mile long, but this is beyond awkward. I just hope my leggings aren't stretched so thin he can see my Wonder Woman panties. Actually, I hope for a whole lot more, but the world opening up and swallowing me doesn't seem as attainable.

He squats and hooks his hands under the treadmill, looks down at me, and says, "Ready?"

"Yeah."

He grunts and lifts. The strain on his muscles has me cringing. The machine must weigh a ton. I'm distracted by his bulging abs when my feet move. Like a tightly stretched spring suddenly let go, I snap free.

Right into Dax's groin.

The treadmill drops with a thud, shaking the floor. Dax collapses to his knees, groaning. I flop on my belly, my legs bouncing when they hit the floor.

I'm never coming back here again.

"Sorry." My apology squeaks from where I've buried my face in my arms.

So much for staying off his radar.

Chapter Eight

-Dax-

Shifting in my office chair, I adjust the ice pack between my legs, then rewind the recording of the security feed back to Rory's epic fail. I shouldn't, really shouldn't, but I have to watch it at least once before I delete it.

After the debacle, she left without working out. Hopefully, she doesn't let this stop her from coming, even though she mostly just types on her phone while walking on the treadmill. I let her know people fly off those things all the time, but it might not be enough to convince Scaredy Cat Meow.

"Payton, that was below the belt," I grumble and shift in my seat again, not sure what has me more uncomfortable, my bruised body or conscience.

I haven't called her Meow since the fourth grade when I realized what a jerk I was being, even if the name fit. She didn't roar, never has. So, why call her Rory?

My gaze drifted from the screen, so I snap it back. I

need to get this deleted before Tony comes in and reviews the video log. On the screen, she's walking past me, so I stop the rewind and press play. I watch a different camera angle and smirk at how she's totally trying to avoid looking at me.

Deciding this morning to resume my normal workout, even with the interruption, didn't go like I'd planned. I'm not big on showing off. It's why I come in at such an early time, so I'm competing with no one but myself. But Rory keeps arriving earlier and earlier, so I couldn't adjust my routine anymore.

I find the camera closest to the treadmill and huff out a breath of disappointment I wasn't aware of holding. It's obvious she couldn't care less about what I'm doing. That shouldn't prick as much as it does.

Shaking my head, I move the cursor to the top of the screen. Why am I wasting my time with this? With her? Just delete the section and move on.

In the video, her head snaps toward me, and I freeze. That look on her face isn't one of indifference. Some might say its admiration. Suddenly, I wouldn't mind her gazing at me like that always.

She whooshes off the track and tumbles to the floor. I bark out a laugh and cue it back to watch again. Sitting back in my chair, I let the video play through, laughing even louder at the look of agony on my face when her foot makes contact. It's fitting, really, when I think back on what a jerk I used to be.

My phone rings, and I pause my third time through watching. The video stops right when I get a punt to the family jewels. I'm chuckling as I answer without looking at who the caller is.

"Yep."

"Dax, that you?" The brisk tone of Vince Stoll, the president of the investment group I'm hoping will take Bodies in Motion to the next level, jerks me to focus.

Once again, I've let Aurora Wilde distract me.

"Yes, sir. Good morning." I push back from the desk and gaze out the window.

He snickers. "I wasn't sure. I thought I heard you laughing. But Dax Payton never laughs or has fun. Doesn't have time for it, right?"

"Something like that."

I force a chuckle and stand. His comment has my skin tight—constricting, like there's a crank in my back twisting my skin in. I have plenty of fun.

"Well, good. That's what makes you a good investment, son." Another whirl of the crank, and my entire body tightens.

I bounce on my toes and roll my shoulders. I'm just off from not being able to have my space and time in the morning. The week has been one giant spiral since day one of Rory's invasion.

"Speaking of, we'd like you to come down to New York for a chat." This is it. They're finally ready to invest.

Every nerve ending hums.

"I can do that. When do you want to meet?"

"We have our annual summer golf tournament with the board and their families out at Martha's Vineyard this weekend. Basically, a chance for us to drink and eat too much while the wives shop and gossip. Why don't you plan on joining us for part of it?" Vince's question's rhetorical.

This request isn't optional.

My heart sinks. That weekend's the first tournament

for the junior rugby team I coach. I've been preparing the kids for it all winter and spring. I can't miss it.

But I can't let this investment opportunity pass, either.

Movement draws my attention from the window. Tony nods as he saunters through the door with a donut in one hand and a to-go cup from the Rez in another. I'm going to have to leave the team's win up to Tony.

"Sounds like a weekend I don't want to miss." I swallow the lump in my throat.

"Great," Vince says at the same time as Tony's eyes hit the computer screen.

His face splits into unrestrained glee. "Is that Meow Wilde?"

I wave him off, pointing to the phone up to my ear, but he sits in my chair and cues the video back.

"Dax, you still there?" Vince asks.

"Yeah. Sorry. An employee didn't realize I was on a call." I kick the chair to get Tony away from the computer, but he anticipates my move and secures himself to the desk.

Having my best friend as my manager's a mistake.

"I'll have my assistant send you the information." All jesting has left Vince's voice, and he's down to business. "We're looking forward to talking with you, Dax."

Tony giggles like a schoolgirl, and I kick the chair again.

"I have high hopes for you, son," Vince adds, but I hate how he calls me that.

It's patronizing. There was no one holding my hand while I built this business from the frozen Alaskan ground up. Nope. It's a product of my grit and determination.

I push my annoyance to the side. "Thanks, sir."

"See you next weekend." With that, Vince hangs up.

I toss the phone on the desk. It hasn't even landed, and Tony erupts into full-on donkey laughter. He's laughing so hard he's crying.

"Would you quiet down?" I cross to the door, slam it shut, and lock it for good measure.

"Man, this is amazing." He clicks the mouse, and the video plays back with sound this time.

He's cued it right to moment of impact. My half scream, half groan fills the office.

"I'm so posting this on TikTok, Instagram, YouTube ... everywhere!" Tony laughs as he's clicking away.

"No," I growl, reaching across the desk and slamming my hand onto his.

"Man, this is classic. Better than classic. This fail right here's epic." The look Tony gives me screams he thinks I'm nuts.

"You're not posting it. It's disappearing. Permanently." I stalk around the desk.

"No!" The incredulity on his face would be amusing if this wasn't so important.

"Yes. This doesn't leak. Period."

I emphasize my point with a shove on the chair. He's so disappointed he doesn't even stop it as he wheels across the office and slams into the filing cabinet. I turn to the computer and select the time section of the incident.

"Dax, wait. Think about this for a second." Tony snaps out of his stupor. "This could be used for good publicity."

I scoff.

"Really. Please, just … wait." He pushes my shoulder to get me to turn around.

With a huff, I face him and cross my arms. I position myself in front of the computer so he doesn't get any crazy ideas.

"Listen. We put this up on social media, and you'll go viral, man. Sure, it's funny as all get-out, but … look at you, Dax. You're a total beast. People will laugh, yes, but they'll also see you and want the same." He motions his hands up and down my body, and I relax a bit.

He has a point.

I glance at the screen, and Rory's horrified look and extreme embarrassment comes back to mind. Posting this may help me and Bodies in Motion, but it'd mortify her. Decision made, I shake my head and turn back to the keyboard.

"Not worth it."

"Why? Because you'll be laughed at for getting clocked in the junk drawer?"

"No." After years of rugby, that doesn't bother me. Much.

"Then what?" Tony leans over the edge of my desk.

"Just drop it."

"No, man. We don't get a marketing opportunity like this often. It's gold. Money in the bank." He throws his hands wide. "We've been busting our butts for years growing this business, and you're going to pass up what's essentially a platter of wealth? That's not you, man."

"Think for a second." I pound my fist into the desk to get his attention. "I'm not the only one who'll be a laughingstock."

"Meow?" He scoffs, his face scrunching in a jeer. "Since when did you care about her?"

"Since I grew up and stopped being a jerk." I lean forward. "Maybe you should consider doing the same. And don't call her that."

"We could blur her face."

"No. I'm not taking the chance her identity gets out."

"Who cares? It's not like anyone'll know who she is. She's a recluse. A nobody."

"I care!" I yell, my entire body trembling with rage.

"You, like, got a thing for her or something?" He steps back, shaking his head with a scowl.

"No. Absolutely not," I heave out though my heart pounds against my chest in objection. "I don't want to be a person who uses others' embarrassment to advance myself. That's not the message I want connected to Bodies in Motion." I stand straight and spear him with a glare. "We're not posting it or any other clips of people failing. Ever. That's not us."

"Fine." He stomps out the office. "Take the hard way, like always."

He marks his protest with a slam of the door. I clench my teeth as I delete the video, making sure to erase all traces of it from the computer and cloud. First, I take a kick where it counts, then am issued a summons I can't refuse during a weekend I've been looking forward to all spring. Now, I've angered the only friend I haven't managed to shut out.

I shake my head and slump into the chair. Business requires sacrifice. Right? I'm just not sure how much more I have to give.

Chapter Nine

-Rory-

"Seriously?" I yell at my screen. "Can you just cooperate for once?"

This couple in my work-in-progress has gone from one I was excited to get to know to one I'd like to drop in an active volcano. They're so far off my plot outline they're practically lost in a jungle of tangled nonsense. It wouldn't be so bad if their banter snapped and their personalities didn't suck.

Yes, I'm aware it's me that sucks.

It's much easier on my psyche if I blame the fictional characters I created rather than myself.

"Argh!"

I chuck my stress ball at my office wall in the kennel where I've hung my deadline for motivation. The ball sails out the door, and I cock my eyebrow at the speed it flies. Has lifting a few weights helped my throw? Too bad it hasn't improved my aim. A dog yips, and nails click in a frantic run to get the projectile.

Chub's snore softly vibrates at my feet.

"Rory, what's wrong?" Sadie rushes into the room. Her wirehaired pointing griffon, Rowdy, follows her and drops my stress ball at her feet. "Is it the kennel?"

"No. The kennel's fine."

Now.

I still haven't told my sister and cousins that I've been secretly using my book money to keep the kennel afloat. So many secrets. I take a deep breath and push back from the desk, shoving my conscience away as well. My family never would've let me use my book money for the kennel, especially not as much as I did.

But I couldn't let their dream of having this place that specializes in training and breeding search-and-rescue and law-enforcement dogs fail. It was all they had talked about growing up.

"What's wrong with the kennel?" Denali walks up, and Sadie moves into my office to make room.

"Nothing." I don't have time for this. My deadline looms in the not-so-distant future, mocking me. "Nothing's wrong with the kennel."

"So, what has you chucking tennis balls and screaming like a banshee?" Sadie pulls out one of the chairs in front of my desk and sits.

Denali takes the other chair.

I'm not sure how I manage to suppress the groan of frustration with them settling in. My restraint's award worthy.

"I'm just having writer's block is all." I wave my hand in the air like it's no big deal.

"Still can't believe my only sister didn't tell me she's this amazing author." Denali crosses her arms over her chest.

She's been more upset about this than I thought she'd be.

"I know. I'm sorry … again."

I've already explained my reasoning until I felt like an orca stuck under the surface, not able to come up for air. Yet, I can't blame her. Our family's tight and shares everything.

Too much sometimes.

I will never tell her a big part of the reason I kept my writing a secret so long is because I didn't want to rub it in her face that I got to chase my dream when she had to lose hers. When she got pregnant her senior year with Sawyer, Denali put her future on hold to raise him. We all banded together to help her, but she took the brunt of the consequences. If she could go back in time, she'd still have Sawyer.

He's that awesome.

I just feel guilty for being able to do what I always wanted to when she had to give so much up to be a single parent.

"No more secrets." Denali glares and points at me.

"Scouts honor." I hold up two fingers on my right hand and cross two on my left under the desk.

Great.

Let's just pile more guilt on while I'm at it. I'll do my best to let them in on what's going on right now. Telling them about past secrets, like me single-handedly supporting the kennel while we started up and making the bookkeeping look like I wasn't, won't do anything but cause hurt and upset.

"So, writer's block's an actual thing?" Sadie scoops a handful of Reese's Pieces from my candy dish and pops them in her mouth.

"Yep, and I've——"

My phone rings on my desk where it's sitting right in front of Denali. She smiles and answers the call, putting it on speaker. "Hey, Emmy. You're on speaker. What trouble are you getting into today?"

We all not-so-secretly envy Emmy and her laissez-faire lifestyle. All of us girls were a bit wild growing up. Well, everyone else but me. I just went along with the wild. Emmy beat every one of us hands down. Every time we get together for the weekend, I'm honestly scared what she'll come up with for us to do.

"Ugh. Nothing. Bradley has me organizing the storage room. So, I've strung up a hammock between the shelves, and I'm taking a break. What are you up to?"

"Rory was just going to tell Sadie and I about her writing woes."

"She finally told you?" Emmy's shocked gasp has both Sadie and Denali glaring at me. "Wait a sec. I'm hanging up so we can video chat."

The phone goes silent. So does the room as they both look ready to kill me.

"She knew, and we didn't?" Denali asks, her hurt spearing me in the heart.

I clear my throat, cringe, and nod. "Sorry."

"You're in so much trouble." Sadie leans back in her chair with a huff.

I close my eyes. "I know."

The video chat rings, and I prop the phone against the candy dish so Emmy can see everyone. She's in a hammock with a table set up next to her with a drink and bag of jerky. The storage room behind her is an absolute mess.

"Remind me never to ask for your help cleaning." I gawk at the equipment tumbled behind her.

"Ever," Sadie deadpans, drawing my smile up for the first time all morning.

"Yeah, well, I'm reorganizing." Emmy grabs her drink and settles into her hammock.

"Clearly." I force a laugh, but it comes out more a nervous chuckle.

"How'd the big secret come out?" Emmy wags her eyebrows. "Give me all the juicy details."

"No juicy details to give. Violet and Kemp were trying to talk themselves out of trouble with their fake engagement—"

"Which I still can't believe they're trying to pull off. It never works in your books." Emmy shakes her head like she's disappointed, but the huge grin stretched across her face negates the action. "How jealous are we that they're going on this awesome adventure?"

"Totally," Denali and Sadie say at the exact same time, then burst into giggles.

I'm too stressed to be jealous.

Or amused.

I really need to get these guys out of here so I can go back to pulling my hair out over a manuscript that should be deleted. My mouth stays shut, though. I don't want to hurt their feelings even more.

"So, they were just talking about the race and your books came up?" Emmy asks.

"No. Sawyer figured it out long ago and let it slip."

"Of course, he did. That kid's a certifiable Einstein." Emmy shakes her head. "Well, I'm glad the cat's out of the bag. Do you know how hard it's been not telling you all how I'm the inspiration behind all Rory's awesomeness?"

"You aren't all of it," I grouse.

She ignores me and looks at Denali and Sadie. "I told her I wasn't going to help her with story ideas until she got out of her bubble. Her muse's probably bored out of her mind being stuck in the same routine week after week." Emmy really knows how to hit someone where it counts. "How's the problem book baby going?"

"Not good, if her screaming and throwing stuff's an indication." Sadie talks around the candy she just tossed in her mouth.

Each clink of candy coating makes me twitch in annoyance.

"Did you take my advice and change things up?" Emmy asks.

"She's going to the gym," Denali answers for me.

Maybe they could keep talking while I take my computer and leave. They obviously don't need me for this conversation.

"And it's not helping?" Emmy's face scrunches in confusion. "What, are the men old and overweight or something?"

Instantly, Dax's stacked abs spring to mind. I took a few days off after the treadmill incident. Wasn't going to go back at all, but I needed to prove to myself that I could push past the embarrassment. Only, the gym has been empty, with no Dax in sight. Now, with the weekend starting tomorrow and me not going to work out on Saturday or Sunday, I won't see him until Monday to confront my shame head on.

Not that I'm complaining.

"Her face is all red, so there has to be at least a few

good-looking guys." Sadie waves her finger toward my face like she's examining it.

"There's guys." Or one guy, really, but I'm not about to tell them that.

"Then you're going to have to do more." Emmy climbs out of her hammock and paces. "Just going to the gym isn't enough."

"What do you mean 'more?'" My skin tingles like my Spidey sense activated.

"You need real adventure. Not just running on a treadmill." Emmy's remark sends all those tingles to explode in another blush.

"Is that all you do there?" Denali asks.

I'll go to my grave before I tell them about my mortifying mishap.

"No. I lift weights." Occasionally, when I don't run out of time.

"Ladies, focus," Emmy snaps. Rich coming from the self-proclaimed Queen of ADHD. "Where can we find her some action? Something that will snap her out of her funk and get her creative juices flowing again?"

"She can come with me and Bjørn in the helicopter. We take the dogs on training runs at least once a week." Sadie scoots forward on her chair.

"Training missions aren't going to cut it." Emmy dismisses the suggestion.

I'm glad I don't have to tell them I'm terrified of flying in that hunk of metal Sadie's fiancé flies. I don't doubt he's a great pilot. One doesn't become a member of the super elite Night Stalker regiment of the military being subpar. Yet, after their crash onto the rocky cliff last year while out saving a bunch of teens, I've added helicopters to my list of things too dangerous to try.

"You know, maybe I just need to accept that I'm tapped out. I could probably pivot and write children's books or something." I push my glasses up on my head and press the heels of my hands into my eyes.

Kid lit would be safer and more my pace anyway.

"Are you kidding me?" Emmy yells, her arms flailing with the phone still in her hand.

The chaos makes me motion sick.

"You write the most amazing books, Aurora Wilde, and you won't quit." Emmy settles down and spears me with an expression that's meant to intimidate through the camera.

It works.

"You have a way of pulling the reader into the story and making them feel like they're right there with the couple fighting against whatever struggle you've put against them." Emmy's on a roll today. "There're times I'll read the entire book straight through, and you all know I can't focus on anything for that long."

"That's the truth," Denali inserts with a snort.

"Right. So, the fact that me, a person who's not a fan of reading, gets sucked into your books and don't want to leave is proof you're a great writer." Emmy leans against an empty shelf. "You need to find some excitement, and not going to train dogs and watch Sadie make googly eyes at her hunk of a fiancé."

Sadie gasps. "I don't make googly eyes."

"Yes, you do," all three of us respond.

This time I do laugh. And it feels good.

Better than good.

It's relief.

"So, how do I find excitement?" I'm afraid to ask.

"You need adventure, a date, anything that stretches

you more than what you're getting at the gym." Emmy chuckles at her pun. "Get it? Stretches."

All of us roll our eyes.

"And you can't just go with Mark." Denali crosses her arms with a nod.

"Why not with Mark? We have fun together," I ask and quickly tack on so they don't get the wrong idea. "Not that we'd go on a date, but we could do some kind of adventure, maybe sea kayak or something."

She shakes her head as I talk. "You're too comfortable with him. He's safe and will never be more than just friends to you."

"Much to his dismay," Sadie adds.

"Totally," Emmy and Denali say as I gape at them.

I didn't think his attraction to me was that obvious. I've done a pretty good job at ignoring it exists. If I acknowledge it, even to these guys, then our friendship will change.

"What in the world are you talking about?" I think I pull off pretending I don't know.

Denali sighs long and loud, making those spidey tingles turn to hordes of baby spiders running along my skin. "He's been in love with you since eighth grade, Rore."

"No. You're wrong," I continue to play dumb, but my stomach twists as they all nod and look at me in pity.

How could they've known since way back then? I just figured it out myself a few years ago.

I groan and bury my face in my hands and flop onto my desk. "I don't need this right now."

And I don't mean about Mark. I don't need any of this nonsense about adventures. I just need to get the book finished, and I can't do that with them yapping at me.

"Don't worry about it. It's not like anything has to change between you." Sadie places her hand on my head. "He's still your best friend, and he's happy with that role. Otherwise, he wouldn't be hanging around."

"All righty." Emmy claps. "Now, that we've got another cat out of the bag, we need to figure out how to help Rory put the wild back in our last name. She needs more than just an 'e.' Us Wilde's are more than eh." Her focus's laser sharp today.

Pity.

I have no clue where to find adventure and finding a date's even more elusive. Haven't had luck in that area of life since … well, forever. I've a sinking feeling if my writing career hinges on me getting a date, it's toast.

Chapter Ten

-*Dax*-

Ice clinks in amber-filled glasses around me. Voices talk over each other in a bid for dominance. Since arriving at Martha's Vineyard this morning, I've had to listen to the members of the investor board as they jostle for position. It started over Bloody Mary's and omelets at breakfast, furthered with sipping craft beers while smacking balls down the green, and continues now in the semi-private room of the golf course's clubhouse. While mostly good-hearted, it's exhausting and a waste of my time.

Slowly, so I don't draw attention to myself, I take a deep breath as I gaze at the sunset reflected on the lake just outside the window. The view has nothing on the mountains that jut straight from the ocean back in Seward. I'm ready to get this meeting over with and get back home where the air doesn't stick to my body and I don't have to fake being friendly.

I take a drink of my ice water, but it doesn't help the general sweltering heaviness that hit me the instant I stepped from the plane. I had hoped taking a few days to visit my other gyms would help me come to the meeting filled with confidence. It worked, mostly. Pride and disbelief still fill me with awe every time I walk into one of the gyms.

If the board and I could've gotten straight to the point and talked shop, I would've taken that wonderment rushing through my veins and inspired them to empty their coffers into mine. But now, after a long day of small talk, I'm irritated. Not a good headspace to be in when the entire future of Bodies in Motion is on the line.

Okay.

That's a little dramatic.

We'd be fine without the money from the investors. I just wouldn't be able to expand nationwide at the speed I want.

"Sure you don't want something with a bit more bite than water, son?" Vince asks for at least the fourth time today.

I force a smile and lift my glass toward him. "It's the elixir of life, Vince." I shrug. "Plus, I'm allergic to alcohol."

True, but not in the break-into-hives, throat-closing sense of the word. After surviving childhood with my father, just the thought of not being in control of my body and actions makes me itch. There's no way I'm letting that poison pass my lips.

"You don't drink. You're a horrible golfer." He *tsks* and shakes his head. "I'm beginning to wonder about you, Payton."

The cronies around the table snicker, turning eager eyes on Vince. It's clear who the alpha male of this group is. All the blustering through the day was just play. Vince rules the pack. Everyone else falls behind his lead.

"Not a lot of opportunity for golf up in Alaska." I set my water on the table, lean back in the lounge chair, and cross one ankle on my knee.

I'm not about to challenge his leadership. But I'm also not going to show weakness. This lone wolf knows the power in holding my own. Men like Vince won't respect anything less.

"Besides, finding golf clubs for someone like me is nearly impossible." Not that I've really searched that hard.

"Speaking of that, how tall are you, Dax?" Clay, the only man I'd enjoyed conversing with all day, asks.

"Just shy of six-six."

Whistles sound around the room.

"Where do you get your clothes, Goliaths R Us?" Clay's easygoing manner puts me a little at ease.

"Something like that."

His presence in this good ol' boys' club surprised me. He can't be much older than forty, a good twenty years and more younger than the rest of the bunch. He lacks the pretentiousness of the others too. How did someone like him get into a group like this? Either he inherited his position or he's worth a fortune.

"Hopefully, it'll take more than a tiny stone to take you down." Vince sips his bourbon, staring me down over the top of his glass.

"No worries there." I hold his gaze. "I've had boulders tossed my way and busted through."

"With a physique like yours and your hard work, I don't doubt it." Clay claps his hand on my shoulder.

"It's mighty impressive what you've been able to build from a speck of nothing in that small town in Alaska."

Vince's gaze darts to the younger man, his eyes narrowing a bit. Either he doesn't like someone else taking the lead, or he's worried Clay will show too much of their hand. Whatever the case, I can't afford Vince getting his boxers in a bunch.

"Lots of grit and ingenuity in Alaska. The country demands it for survival. I didn't want to just survive, though. I wanted to thrive, like Vince here," I nod at him, and the man's chest puffs with pride.

Flattery always appeases the alpha.

Especially ones like Vince.

"We like you, son. Not gonna beat around the bush about that." Vince points his glass at me, then sets his bourbon on the table. "It's no secret you've got something special."

"Thank you."

"To create what you have at such a young age impresses us. Finding your kind of drive and vision's hard." All good so far, but Vince sits back in his chair and mirrors my position.

A drop of sweat beads at the top of my back. He's building up to something, I can tell.

"The thing is, gyms are a dime a dozen."

I clench my teeth together to keep my retort in. I know that he knows Bodies in Motion stands apart from the rest. If it didn't, I wouldn't be wasting the day chitchatting with a bunch of elitists in their private club. But all my life I've dealt with men like Vince who throw their weight around to get what they want. I know when to keep my mouth shut.

When I don't rise to the bait, he continues,

"Granted, yours is a mighty spectacular dime, but it's still a dime."

They aren't going to give me funding. The realization hits me, and the anger I spent so many years learning how to harness rumbles under my skin. Why make me come all the way out here and dance to their tune if they weren't interested?

"Listen, son." If he calls me son one more time, I'm reaching over this table. "We want to invest in Bodies in Motion, in you, but we need to see that there's more there than just a bunch of jocks getting stacked."

So, they're not turning me down?

"Okay." I lift an eyebrow. "Just what are you hoping to see?"

I'm open to suggestions, as long as it doesn't compromise the mission of Bodies in Motion. I don't want my gyms turning into places only people like Vince and his cronies would go to, Clay aside. I'd workout with him any day.

"Your business is top notch, Dax, but that's not what will make all of us millions. You will." Vince steeples his hands like he's The Godfather or something.

"I don't understand." And I hate that I have to admit that.

"The real potential for greatness isn't the gym. That's secondary to you. The only way that Bodies in Motion will ever become a nationwide brand is if you become the next American workout guru. Granted, we're already seventy percent there with you being who you are, *if* people saw you. You personally have absolutely no social media presence. I mean, the women will buy whatever you sell just to watch you flex your muscles, and yet you're nowhere to be found." Vince chuckles and motions to the pack to join.

They do, like a bunch of hyenas.

"I see." So, they just view me as eye candy to exploit. "I'm not big on parading around, showing off."

"That's not what we're wanting, either," Clay insists.

I turn to him, not able to look at Vince's smug face any longer.

"You said that you have a program you're working on that could change people's lives." Clay leans forward like he's really interested and not just seeing dollar signs.

"Yeah. I've done years of research and have first-hand experience with getting my body to its peak potential, but it's more than that. It's looking at brain and soul health as well. A toned body's worth squat if your cognitive and mental health tank."

Theoretically, I know I'm right. I just haven't taken the next step to test it on someone else.

"Exactly. Imagine helping people across the nation —shoot, around the world—with your program. Not only will it cause a revolution in fitness, but it's marketable on a grand scale." Clay holds his hands open.

I'm starting to see the vision.

"Supply and demand, son." Vince ruins the moment. "A gym has limits in how much money it can make us. You, however, are limitless."

I lift a hand toward Vince for him to proceed. His lip twitches in satisfaction.

"If you can prove this program of yours works, we're willing to back the Bodies in Motion brand. We'll give you the money you need to open your next hundred gyms, plus the funds necessary to produce and market

Get Ripped with Dax Payton or whatever you want to call this whole body, soul, and mind mumbo jumbo you've got going on."

It's huge.

More than I had hoped for.

So, why do I feel sick to my stomach?

"How do you want me to prove it?" I ask, keeping my muscles loose so he can't see my discomfort.

"Find someone to practice on. Take them from zero to hero in three months, and you've got our backing."

I blow out a breath. "Three months isn't very long."

"Son, this world's all about instant gratification. Your little program takes more time than that and no one will fork out their money for it," Vince scoffs.

"And your terms?"

He reaches for his bourbon and motions nonchalantly. "Just your normal percentage for a major contribution." He takes a slow drink, obviously reveling in his power. "If you're serious about taking your business to the next level and finding financial freedom, I have our investment offer all drafted and ready to email."

I hate that I have to even consider aligning my business with this man, but in order to move forward, I need to take big risks. Besides, it's the investor group I'll be working with, not just him. As a whole, their track record for finding businesses with potential and exploding them is incomparable.

"Send it to me." I stretch my hand across the table.

His grin's like the Cheshire cat's, all oily and supercilious. When his hand clamps in mine, I swear my skin crawls from the contact. I shake off the feeling. Just because I don't like Vince, doesn't mean the offer won't be exactly what my business needs.

Chapter Eleven

-Rory-

Staring into the empty fireplace hasn't helped me come up with either a fix to my plot mess or a way to conjure up a man. I'm no further from "eh" then I was two hours ago. If anything, I'm more "eh" than ever.

"Grr. Seriously, Chub. It can't be this hard!" I turn to him where he's lying on the other couch cushion.

He moans a huff.

"You're right. If it was easy, my manuscript would practically write itself, and my phone would be ringing off the hook with men desperate for me."

My phone vibrates and rings Jodi's tone. Oh, thank goodness. Maybe she'll have some ideas.

"Finally. I can't tell you how happy I am that you aren't camping on some stupid mountain with your husband anymore." I go into our normal teasing when she's been gone. "Tell him you're not allowed to go out of service until I get my book done."

"That bad?" she asks, but her voice doesn't hold the normal laughter my kidding usually brings.

"Worse. My cousin won't help me anymore. She says I need adventure or a date. Probably both." I mock Emmy's voice. "Oh, and my family found out about me writing. They're all hurt that I kept it a secret so long, which I hate."

"Well, your cousin might be onto something."

"Maybe."

"Sorry about your family," she whispers.

Out of anyone, Jodi knows how hard I've worked to get where I am. She's been in the trenches of the publishing world with me. While she hadn't agreed with me keeping it all hush-hush, she understood. We have the weekend workshop we went to on the Enneagram and how to use it for characters to thank. Part of the class was taking the test ourselves. She got the fun, vivacious Enthusiast, and I wound up with the Peacemaker, never wanting to rock the boat and make waves.

"Listen, I really hate to tell you this, but I know you don't do social media so much …" Her hesitation sends dread tumbling through me.

"What? What's going on now?"

My voice is all airy and trembling like the girls in scary movies when the bad guy's hiding and about to jump out and attack. Silly, really. Whatever Jodi's about to say isn't life or death.

"That reviewer from Goodreads has an entire social media presence around her reviews."

"No."

Great.

This is worse than death.

"Yeah. Her videos always go viral."

"No, no, no!" I push to the edge of the couch

cushion and put her on speaker so I can open my app and see for myself. "How bad is it?"

"Well, honestly, I don't know, Rore. I've never seen anything like this before."

Her response doesn't make me feel any better. She's the queen of Social Media Land, where I'm the leper, staying well away from the city walls. How can I combat something the queen isn't even aware of?

I click open the folder on my phone where I put all the media apps for that one day a month I post something then slink away. My finger hovers over the apps. I'm so overwhelmed, I don't know where to look.

"How do I find it?" I can't hide the shaking in my voice.

"Here, I'll send it to you," Jodi says.

Two seconds later, my phone beeps with a text. I open it, then watch in horror as a woman I've never met or even heard of rips me apart. She's moved on from *Washed Out* to my other books. The video's flashy, with sound effects and short, cut-in videos of dogs pooing. Tears stream down my face.

"This is—" A sob cuts off my words.

"Disgusting. I know," Jodi inserts, though I'm not sure what word I'd use. "I promise you, Rore, this isn't how the reader community is. You know I love being on these apps and interacting. This isn't normal."

"Then why does she have such a following?" I blubber out. "This video has over a million views!"

Chub whines, gets up, and lays his head on my lap.

"I've looked through the comments, and most of them are from people who aren't part of the reading community, and the ones that are stick up for you," Jodi insists.

I pull up the hundreds of comments and scroll through them. "How can you even tell?"

"I spent the last hour clicking on profiles and basically trolling the jerks."

"Why would she do this?"

I swipe my finger on the screen and go to her other videos. She has hundreds, all roasting different books and authors.

"Some people are just mean. They use the platforms to make themselves stars, and the easiest way to do that is pull other people down. But I don't think this is all bad."

"How could this not be all bad? This is beyond horrible." I close the app, ease Chub's head off my leg, and stand.

"Listen, she'll move on to someone else soon. That seems to be her M.O. In the meantime, you're getting free advertising, and I'd bet you've had a spike in sales." Jodi's rational doesn't matter.

"I don't want a spike if it's people who would read only to be nasty."

I stalk to my kitchen, jerk open the freezer, and snatch a Haagan Daz bar. As I close the door, I second-guess myself and pull out the entire box. This is definitely a binge ice cream and wallow moment.

"I know you don't, sweetie. I know. She shouldn't be able to build a platform on something like this." Jodi sighs. "But, there're only a few things you can do about it."

"Which are?" I ask around my mouthful of ice cream.

"Combat it with videos of your own. You could lean into what she's saying, making fun of yourself and your writing while showing that you're a bigger person compared to her suckiness."

"Are you kidding me?"

Jodi talks over my outburst. "Or you can ignore it. Pretend it never happened, be happy about the increase in royalties, and move on."

"Those are horrible choices."

"I know."

"Why do I do this again? Why slog through writing just to be torn down? I'm not sure I remember anymore." I twirl the ice cream bar in my fingers, my vision blurring with tears as I stare at it.

"You do it because you're a storyteller, and a right good one too," Jodi says with force. "Not doing so would be like asking the birds not to sing."

"Cheesy." I roll my eyes.

"Darn. I was going for inspirational," Jodi shoots back.

She's right, though. I can't imagine life without writing. It's been my identity, my comfort and the one thing I could claim as unique, for so long. Without writing, I'm just a lonely, pathetic woman with a lazy dog.

Chapter Twelve

-Dax-

No matter how many mornings I spend gazing out this window at the bay, I'm still awestruck by the mountains shooting from the ocean into the sky and the hard-working fisherman motoring past to dangerous waters. I often toss around the idea of moving to one of the other gyms and making that my base. It'd be more convenient getting to the other gyms and growing not having to take several flights, costing more hours and money than necessary.

I just can't.

Being away from here would be losing the energy that fuels and regenerates me.

I inhale, then calmly shift out of sun salutation to warrior pose. After the long flights home and tossing and turning the remaining of the night away, I need this slower start before I get serious. Need the chance to slow my brain from thinking about Vince's challenge and the investor group's terms.

The door clicks, and Rory whooshes in. Her moves

are jerky and forceful as I watch in the window's reflection. Her bag catches in the closing door, whipping her to a stop. She yanks it free, and a loud ripping sound reaches all the way to me.

"Great," she mutters and turns around, freezing when she sees me. "Perfect."

Her shoulders slump as she stomps to the stair master. Guess she's given up on the treadmill. I was hoping my time away had given her a chance to get over her embarrassment. She doesn't look my way, so I guess I hoped in vain.

"Morning." I've no right to expect civility from her, not with how I tormented her through school, and, after the treadmill incident, I'm shocked she's still here.

She startles and turns toward me. Her eyes are red-rimmed and puffy. Something's wrong, and all my protector instincts honed from years of deflecting my father's abuse of my mom toward me flare to life. Rich considering I was Rory's antagonist growing up.

"Morning," she mumbles and rushes to the machine.

She doesn't want or need my protection. I don't need the distraction, either. Not with three months until the guillotine drops. Focusing back on the ocean, I exhale into reverse warrior.

Pounding sounds to my left, followed by her frustrated, "Stupid, fancy junk machine." She pushes more buttons as she stands on the immobile stair. "Just start."

With the last word, she hits the side of her fist on the console. The machine comes to life at a speed she wasn't ready for. She runs as the stairs circle. Her hands grip the rails to hold her up. Every time she lets go to reach toward the console she stumbles, almost falling.

I rush across the gym, stretching my stride to get

there faster. Leaping over the machine next to hers, I slam my hand on the kill switch. The stairs stop, and she folds her body over as she catches her breath. My own chest heaves with adrenaline like I just played a grueling rugby match on the pitch.

A laugh tickles my throat, threatening to escape. I swallow it down and press my lips tight together to keep it in. Laughing now would make this situation so much worse.

"I give up." She sucks in a shuddering breath. "I'm done. Done with these stupid machines. Done with evil women and their nasty reviews. I'm done."

She slides herself down until she's sitting on the stair. I don't even think she remembers I'm right here. Tears stream down her cheeks. Her glasses sit askew on her blotchy face. Yet, even crying, she's beautiful.

"This isn't helping. How can I ever expect to go on stupid adventures, let alone with a man, if I can't even walk on circling stairs?" She definitely doesn't remember I'm here, or she's so distressed she doesn't care.

Aurora Wilde would never in her right mind spew words like that in front of me. Not with how past me would have used them against her. Not wanting to startle her, I hold still where I lean with my hands on my knees. Maybe if she can get out whatever's bothering her, she'll be able to get back to her workout?

"I'm weak. Boring," she spits out as a sob shakes her shoulders. "I just need to accept that and stop pretending. My characters'll languish in the jungle of mediocre writing, and I'll become the town's crone with nothing but my flower beds and lazy dog to keep me company."

I hate that she's putting herself down.

"No, you're not," I practically growl.

She shrieks and twists to me. Yep. She forgot all about me.

Her face falls, and she buries it into her hands. "See. I just blabbed my weaknesses to the enemy."

"Really? Can't we move past when I was an immature idiot?" I huff as I stand.

"No," she snaps.

"Fair enough." It stabs, but I don't blame her. "Don't sell yourself short. You're not crone material."

She barks an airy laugh, then sniffs. "I just need help."

A light bulb pops on in my head. If she wants to get strong, she can be my test subject. I move in front of her and take a knee so I'm at her level. I'm all about getting rid of weakness.

I swallow the rock in my throat and say the words neither of us ever imagined coming out of my mouth. "I can help you."

Her face morphs from surprise to horror behind her still-crooked glasses. "You want to take me on adventures?"

"What?" I have no clue what she's talking about, but now that the idea's planted in my head, I wouldn't mind showing perfectly laced Rory Wilde some excitement. "You whined about being weak."

Smooth, Payton. Real smooth.

"I couldn't care less about working out." She motions with her hands at the gym. "All this was a ploy to snap me out of my funk so I can write again."

"You're a writer?" I had a suspicion when I was reading a book a few years back, but I want her to confirm it.

"Yes. Since my family now knows, might as well blab

it to the world." She's muttering and not really making any sense since it's just the two of us.

"You thought coming to the gym would help you write?" I get that. Movement helps your brain function better.

"Yes. No," she groans. "It was my cousin's idea. It failed. *I* failed. Now, she's got an even more ridiculous idea." She scoffs and straightens her glasses as she mumbles on. "Like going hiking or finding a date will suddenly help me write. So. Dumb. I'm done. I'm just … done."

She moves to stand. I shoot to my feet and back up to give her space. My mind races with ideas, but if I don't say it right, she'll bolt. She snatches her bag from the floor, and items fall out of a hole in the side.

"Listen, I'm not sure what you need exactly, but I'm willing to make a bargain with you." My words tumble out of my mouth like her items had from her bag, all fast and flipping.

Her eyebrows push together as she gapes up at me. She shakes her head, shoves a notebook in her bag, and stands. Her arms wrap around the bag to keep everything inside, but it also feels like she's keeping herself together with the action.

"Why would you, Dax Payton, ever make a bargain with me?" My name sounds acidic as she spears me with incredulous eyes.

"Because I need help too." I stick my hands in my pockets to look as relaxed as possible, even though my entire body's tensed like a jack-in-the-box ready to spring free.

"You never need help. Ever." Rory shakes her head.

"No. I just never admit it when I do." I shrug. "I'm trying to get better at that."

She stares at me, disbelief pouring from her eyes as they shift focus from one side of my face to the other. I can't blame her for not trusting me. I've never given her any reason to.

"What would you need help with?" She's actually considering it?

My shock has me shuffling my feet. I think through my words before spewing this time.

"I'm wanting to expand my business to help more people get healthy. It's more than just opening up more gyms. That doesn't actually get people to true health. I've a program I've been working on and an investor group that's interested in backing me, but they want proof that what I want to offer will work."

"So, you need a guinea pig?" One of her eyebrows lifts over her rims.

"Basically."

"And you'd trade helping me if I do this program of yours?" She shifts her bag in her arms.

"Well, you're the perfect candidate with you being so …" I let my words trail off, because I can't think of a word that doesn't have the potential of insulting.

"Clumsy? Fluffy? What am I exactly that makes me so perfect to be your test subject?" She glares at me, but I'm upset that she picks those words to describe herself.

"New, Aurora." I cross my arms and try to tone down my frustration. "You're a complete novice to all of this, so it'll be perfect to show how someone doesn't need to be a fitness junkie for my program to work."

"Oh."

She swallows and closes her eyes. She swallows

again, then shakes her head. When she does open her eyes, she gazes off to the side, not looking at me. A single tear tracks down her cheek.

I grab onto my shirt to keep my arms crossed and my hands to myself. She wouldn't appreciate me reaching up and wiping the tear away. When her chin drops and shoulders slump, my heart plummets into my stomach.

"No. I can't … I can't do this." She steps past me. "I quit."

As she rushes out of the gym, I'm tempted to race after her. Tempted to beg her to reconsider. To forgive me for being a jerk for all those years. I know that's what's holding her back. Can't blame her. If I was her, I wouldn't want to be around me either.

As the door clicks shut behind her, I gaze around the empty gym. Even though I don't know exactly what she needed in return, implementing my program with her would have been perfect. She would have proven that my philosophy works. Sure, I can find someone else. Yet, my disappointment it won't be her drags against me as I stomp to the pull-up bar.

Chapter Thirteen

-Rory-

Yanking open my car door, I toss my bag into the passenger seat next to Chub. Pads of paper, books, pencils, and other junk scatters across my seat and the console. Chub bats his paw at a napkin that lands on his snout, then goes back to sleep. I half growl, half scream as I stomp my feet in a temper tantrum.

"Do you know what he suggested, Chub?" I hastily brush my hand across the seat to clear it and slump in. "He thinks we can help each other and that I'll just sweep all our past under the rug and trust him." I scoff. "As if."

Except, he had owned up to being a jerk in school. Past Dax never did that before. I bite my lip as possibilities whirl.

"No. I can*not* seriously be considering this." I shake my head, but I can't bring myself to find my keys in the mess of junk and leave.

What other options do I have? I don't want to quit writing. Don't even want to quit working out, despite the machines raging against me. But working with Dax Payton's a huge mistake.

Risky.

I'd have to keep what we're doing a secret because my family and friends, well, Mark primarily, would flip. This man single-handedly created every child's school nightmare for me. It took years for people to stop calling me Meow or Scaredy Cat. He took my awkward, introverted self and shoved me even further into the locker of self-doubt.

Bargaining with him should be completely out of the question.

"Totally not an option. I can't do it, Chub." I dig through my bag's contents, locate my keys, and jab them into the ignition.

The engine fires to life and P!nk's song *Courage* blares through the speakers. I squeeze my eyes shut to the fresh tears that sting my face. I don't want to give up. Running's the opposite of brave. It's letting my past continue to control me.

"Can I do this, Chub?"

He lifts his head and rolls to his belly. His chin rests on his front paws as he looks up at me. My vibes must be pretty off if he's willing to interrupt his nap.

"Okay, what's the risk in working with Dax? We're both older now. He seems to have matured, so I really doubt he'll bully me like he did." I tap on the steering wheel. "Okay, bully might be a little strong. Tease and torment, yes, but after elementary school, even that stopped. So, say I do this. Say I let him transform me from a fluffy desk jockey to whatever it is he's going for, will there be a downside?"

Aside from having to engage with Dax? Nothing I

can think of at the moment. I want to be stronger, to maybe even see if there's grace hiding under all the clumsy. Chub moans low.

"Okay, there's very little draw back to being his guinea pig, and if he's a jerk, I'll just leave. I'm not a child stuck in school anymore." I nod, and Chub huffs a breath that shakes his lips.

I'll take that as an agreement.

"And as far as my side of the deal, Dax used to brag all the time about the rock climbing, camping, and back-country snowboarding he was doing. I can't imagine he doesn't do that kind of stuff anymore." I draw in a shaky breath, trying to cleanse the dread any one of those activities conjures up. "He's also surprisingly big on safety. I mean, that was drilled into me at the orientation."

I gnaw on my bottom lip as I consider everything. It's risky, but, according to the girls, that's what I need. Plus, maybe being around my nemesis will spark some good banter.

"Okay, Chub. I'm doing it."

He wags his tail in encouragement. I click the engine off, grab my phone from the pile of junk, and head inside. If I don't go now, I'll lose my nerve.

When I walk through the door, Dax freezes halfway through his pull up. His surprised gaze connects with mine and holds. The hair on the back of my neck stands at attention, and my stomach flips like a silver salmon jumping from the water.

Man, how I hate nerves.

I'm trembling from head to toe as I walk across the gym. His muscles aren't even shaking while he still holds the pull up at the halfway point. When I hit the open workout area, he pulls himself the rest of the way up, slowly lowers, and then saunters toward the middle of the space to meet me.

"I'm willing to consider your offer, even though I'm not particularly fond of you." I cringe.

That was horribly mean. I should apologize. Pulling my shoulders back, I open my mouth, only to be cut off.

"Fair enough." Dax glances out the window then back to me. "What exactly do you need from me?"

His dark gaze spears me, making not just the hairs on my neck rise but the remaining hairs across my skin wave like the northern lights dancing in the sky. This is a bad idea. There's obviously too much history for me to push past if just a look from him makes my skin crawl.

Just be brave, Rory.

"I need to have experiences that push me out of my comfort zone. The novels I write are full of adventure, and I seem to be tapped out of them." I skip over the romance part.

He doesn't need to know that. His eyebrow lifts along with one corner of his mouth. The movement's small, almost imperceptible, but it's there. Mocking me.

"Okay." Dax takes a step closer. "What kind of deal do you want to broker?"

I hadn't thought that far through this plan, and I can't think with him looming over me. My gaze veers to the equipment around us as I pull my bottom lip between my teeth and bite. Whatever we agree to has to benefit us both. I can't sell myself short, with him getting the bulk of the benefits. I'm going to have to think this through more thoroughly before I offer any suggestions.

When I turn my focus back on Dax, he's staring at

my lips. My scalp tingles and cheeks heat. My habit of chewing on myself when I think is so embarrassing. At least I hadn't bitten hard enough to draw blood this time.

I clear my throat, and his eyes snap to mine. "I need time to think about it."

"Think about what?" Dax asks, his brows lowering in confusion.

"Our deal and what exactly I need from it." I cross my arms over my chest, then lower them to my side.

I don't want to appear uncomfortable.

"Right." He nods and rubs his hand across his darkening neck.

Is Dax Payton blushing?

Surely, not.

"I have practice tonight until six. Why don't we meet after to go over our terms?" He crosses his arms, which makes his biceps bulge against his too-tight shirt.

Seriously. Buy a larger size!

"Practice?" I tear my eyes from the fabric strangling his arm.

"I coach junior rugby."

"Oh."

He's still involved with that? I figured he gave it up to be a gym tycoon. Why else would he not be playing professionally like he'd bragged in high school? Hadn't he even gotten a contract with a big team?

"I can swing by your place after practice to discuss how we want to proceed."

I shake my head. There's no way I'm letting him in my sanctuary.

"I can meet you. How about at the field? I've never actually seen rugby played." I can start the whole getting out of my comfort zone off right away. "Unless you'll need to shower or something."

My face heats up. Why would I bring up something like that? It's not like he's trying to impress me or anything.

"Nah. Meeting there should work." He shrugs.

See, he's not worried about being a smelly, tower of sweat.

"And just to show how congenial I can be—"

"Congenial?" I interrupt him with a laugh.

He glares at me. "It means friendly. I thought you were a wordsmith, Aurora."

I roll my eyes and mirror his stance by crossing my arms.

"To show how *friendly* I can be, dinner will be on me." Dax lifts his eyebrow in challenge.

"Fine." I shrug. "Sounds great."

"You bring your terms for me. I'll layout my program to you. If we're both in agreement, we'll start tomorrow. Sound good?" He relaxes his arms to his side.

I do the same. "Perfect."

"All right, then." He takes a step back. "Practice is at the high school football field."

"Great. It's a—" I barely stop myself before I say date. This is nothing of the sort and never will be. "Plan."

I choke out the first word that comes to mind and spin on my heel. The sooner I get out of there, the sooner I can breathe. I push through the door to the crisp morning air and inhale. It doesn't help the nerves circling around my lungs like octopus tentacles.

How could it?

I've just got myself a date with the devil.

Chapter Fourteen

-Dax-

Grunts fill the air as the players ruck up. I peek at my watch, then at the bleachers for the hundredth time. Still no Rory, and it's ten to six.

A whistle blows, snapping my attention back to the pitch where it should be. Agreeing to help Rory was a bad idea. She's already capturing more of my focus than necessary.

Tony instructs the kids on how to adjust the scrum to keep the gate clear so the team can get the ball. At least Tony's paying attention. Maybe having him lead the team in the game the weekend before was a good thing. He tells them to run it again and tosses the ball into the middle of the scrum.

As the players push against each other, Tony saunters toward me, a scowl on his face. "What's up with you today?"

"Nothing."

"Liar." Tony crosses his arms and steps beside me to watch the team practice.

The air around us thickens as we stand in silence. The ball finally gets out of the scrum and is picked up by the eighth-grade rookie, Skye. A car door slams. My head pivots toward the parking lot just as Tony blows his whistle extra loud.

"Rook, we pass sideways or back in rugby. If you can't find someone to toss to, take the hit. If you don't want to take a hit, sign up for pansy football or cheer-leading," Tony yells, then turns to me. "You're off, man."

"Happens." I shrug and call Skye over.

If I don't make a big deal about it, hopefully Tony won't catch on. Having Rory meet me here's a disaster. Not only am I being unfair to my players, but Tony will put more into the meeting than there is.

No more looking at the time or the bleachers.

My team deserves all of me.

Priorities firmly in place, I clap Skye of the shoulder.

"I'm sorry, Coach Payton. Bryce came barreling toward me, and I panicked." She hangs her head.

"Once I had two Samoans from a visiting team steaming at me during a championship tournament. These guys were massive. Built like tanks."

"Bigger than you?" Skye's eyes are wide as she stares up at me.

"I had a good four or five inches on them, but they easily weighed fifty more than me each. And it was all muscle."

"Wow. That'd be scary."

"Yep. It was terrifying." I nod. "Know what I did?"

Her shoulders slump. "You took the hit."

"Nope." I shake my head. "I tossed that ball like it was on fire, right over their heads."

Her head snaps up in disbelief. "Really?"

"Yep. It was pure survival reflex."

"I definitely want to survive."

"Only problem was their team picked up the ball and scored. My desire for self-preservation cost my team the win. In that moment, I valued myself over my team." The shame of that instinct all those years before washes over me like it just happened. "Rugby's a brutal sport. We take harder hits than any other game, don't wear padding, and the clock never stops unless there's an injury or foul play. It's especially hard for you up here in Alaska since we won't have enough players for an all-girl team. I can guarantee that if you continue to play, you'll get injured. I've had more broken bones and sprained muscles than I can remember."

Skye's expression drops and skin pales.

"But, rugby will get into your very soul. There's something about the game of rugby that inspires men and women to be better. Not only will you get smarter and stronger, but you'll learn to trust and be trustworthy. You'll have a community both in your teammates and other players around the world that know the power of hard work and dedication. Rugby isn't just a sport, it's a lifestyle, and it'll be one of the greatest things to ever influence you if you let it, but you have to embrace it, all of it. Because you can't get the good without the bad."

There's a fire in Skye's eyes now. I'm just as rallied by the reminder of what rugby means to me.

"Embrace the suck." Skye nods and claps her hands.

"Exactly." I chuckle and push her toward the field.

For the last ten minutes of practice the kid's a machine. She dodges tackles like a dancer, tosses the ball perfectly at her teammate, then blocks a kid twice her size, holding him long enough for the ball to be carried past the touch line. The team gathers around the player that scored, but Skye gets just as much praise.

I blow my whistle and call them in.

"Take a knee." Once they settle, I scan over each and every one of their faces as I talk. "Good practice, everyone. You're a solid team, backing each other up on the field like you can read each other's minds. No wonder you dominated last weekend on the pitch."

"Oh, man. You missed it, Coach Payton." James, the team captain, bumps his shoulder into Skye next to him.

She teeters but doesn't fall over.

James continues, "Rook here shimmied her way through the breakdown, snatched the ball from under the other forward's nose, and made it halfway down the pitch before the other team even realized she had it."

Skye blushes but just shrugs. "Guess they underestimated me."

"That's an important thing to remember." I point to Skye. "Skye may be the smallest member of the team, but that doesn't mean she's the weakest link. Faf de Klerk's one of the world's elite players, and he's only five-seven. If you all work together and use your strengths instead of just worrying about where you fall short, we'll have a solid team that can win both on the pitch and off."

"Will you be at our next match?" James asks.

"I promise you, I won't miss another." I skim over each of their eyes, making sure they know the depth of my commitment.

They nod or smile. My chest expands like a rugby ball filled with too much air. Before I get mushy, I wave them off.

"Get out of here." As they race past me, I yell. "Don't forget the motto."

"Integrity and honor always, no matter what," they holler back.

A smile splits my face as I turn to watch them go. It disappears when I spy Rory. My pulse kicks into double time at the sight of her standing with a scowl on her face and her arms crossed.

"Ah." Tony snorts. "Now I get it."

"What?" I ask.

"Why your neck snapped to the parking lot so many times I'm sure you have whiplash."

I roll my eyes and walk away.

Unfortunately, he follows. "Thought you said there wasn't anything going on with you and Meow."

"Don't call her that. We aren't in elementary school anymore." I grit my teeth, wishing I could go back in time and just take the stupid lunch she offered me.

"You're really into her, aren't you? And she's okay with that?" Tony grabs my shoulder to stop me.

"Really, Tony, think for once. It's nothing like that." I shake his hand off. "She's agreed to be a guinea pig for our new program. She gets free coaching and saves over a thousand bucks, and I get to prove to the investors the program works. That's it. She's here so I can go over the details. It was the only time we could meet."

I'm not really lying by leaving out half of the deal. There's no reason why Tony needs to know. He'd only make it bigger than it is. I've given him the cliff notes of the investor meeting. He knows how important the next three months are for Bodies in Motion's future.

He glances over to Rory, then spears me with a raised eyebrow. "You sure about that? Because now would be a bad time to be tangling yourself up with distractions."

"Seriously? It's Rory Wilde." I tip my head at her. "There's nothing there, man. Like always."

"If you're sure."

"Don't worry."

I clap him on the shoulder and stomp off. He should know that nothing will happen between me and Rory. Thanks to our past, she'd rather tango with a grizzly than date me. Not that I'd even consider dating her, or anyone. Not now that I'm reeling in my business's future on too light of a weight of fishing line.

Grabbing my duffle of gear and the water cooler, I walk toward the parking lot, not stopping as I get to her. An English bulldog lays at her feet, not moving. If it wasn't for the leash, I'd think the thing was dead.

I inwardly groan the closer I get. Rory has always been pretty without even trying. Over the years, I got really good at not noticing, kind of like how you stop seeing the houses on your street because you drive past every day. That is, until a neighbor paints their door or puts up shutters and you suddenly realize little things have changed at every house.

Well, Rory keeps adding little details to what I've trained myself not to see. That's the only reason my attention veers to her. Like right now, for instance. Her sweater vest over a white dress shirt gives her this whole sexy librarian vibe, and, as a bonafide ink drinker, she's got my eyeballs wanting to guzzle her down.

That won't do.

I nod as I walk on by, not entirely confident my muddled brain won't say something I'll regret.

She huffs in annoyance as I pass.

"Let's go, cupcake," I call back to her. "Daylight's burning."

Not true with the Midnight Sun keeping the sky light most of the night.

"Rory. My name's Rory," she grumbles behind me just loud enough for me to barely hear.

I wish she'd come right out and say it. She's always just taken whatever was dished out to her, whether it was teasing in elementary school or getting the lion's share of the work in group projects in high school. She's never, not once that I can remember, stuck up for herself.

That realization annoys me. Makes me want to push her harder until she blows up at me. Maybe then she'll stop letting others walk all over her.

She steps up beside me, carrying her dog. I snort a laugh and shake my head. She glares up at me. There. There's the start of a fire. My cheek pulls into a one-sided smirk.

"What?" she snaps.

I smother the rest of my mouth's pull into a smile. "Are your dog's legs broken or what?"

"No." She rolls her eyes. "He just won't be able to keep up with your Paul Bunyan stride."

"You know where Two Lakes picnic area is?" I ask.

She flinches. Of course, she does. It's right down the street from her house.

"Hmm. Let me think. I've only lived here my entire life." She hitches the dog in her arms. "I know it. Why didn't you just have me meet you there?"

"Well, after giving it some thought, I figured meeting on neutral territory would be better than having you come to my place. And since I didn't want the rumor mill churning if we were seen at a restaurant, Two Lakes gives us more privacy."

"Oh, dear. That would be bad." Her trembling hand fiddles with her collar.

Her reaction annoys me even more. I stretch my legs wider as I walk, needing space to get my head screwed back on straight.

"Meet you there." I beeline for my truck and take the ten-minute drive to remind myself all the reasons I need to stay focused.

By the time I pull into the parking lot, I'm back on track. I snag the cooler keeping dinner warm and the folder with my program's starter guide I made up today as she parks beside me. Without waiting for her to get her lazy dog, I head toward the gazebo. By the time she gets there, I have steaming smoked pork and sautéed onions piled onto paper plates.

"Let's get to this. We've got an early date tomorrow." I wink at her and motion for her to sit across from me at the picnic table.

She glares, but steps over the bench seat. Her dog slumps to the ground with a tired sigh.

I slide the folder to her and start right in.

"We'll not only be working on building strength, but it'll be an entire body and mind overhaul."

"Great. So, now I'm a car that needs a tune up."

"Not a tune up, cupcake. This is a complete remodel." I fork a mound of pork and take a bite.

Her cheeks tighten like she's gritting her teeth. Instead of coming back with a remark, she flips the folder open. Her eyebrows furrow beneath her turquoise glasses. The faster her eyes scan the document, the further her jaw drops.

"Five days a week?" Her gaze snaps to mine.

I shrug. "It's not like you aren't already doing that."

"Fine." She taps the page. "Only twenty grams of carbs a day? That's like … nothing."

"Pretty much." I stab more meat and lift it toward her. "Healing comes in ketosis. If you want your body performing and recovering at peak capability, if you want your brain to function at its pinnacle—which if you're having trouble writing these books of yours, I'm thinking it's not—then you need to make sure your body's using the best fuel for it. Ketones are a human's best source. You can't make ketones eating cupcakes."

I shove the meat into my mouth and lift an eyebrow in challenge.

"Fine," she grumbles and slams the folder closed. "I'll eat like a Neanderthal."

She takes a small bite and chews. Her wheels turn. I can tell by the way she deliberately stabs meat and onions and slowly chews, all while staring at a spot on the table between us.

"So, I don't have my terms typed and collated. Sorry." She gives me a false smile.

"No worries. I'm pretty good at remembering details." I fork another bite in.

"I'll require new experiences weekly." She sets her utensil on the edge of the plate and pulls her shoulders back.

She's expecting me to disagree.

Will she ever stop assuming the worst of me?

"Go on." Bite. Chew. Pretend I'm not annoyed.

"I'm not talking easy hikes on boardwalk trails." She points to the path weaving off into the trees. "These need to be bonafide adventures. Activities that'll challenge me."

"Like what?" I ask around another bite.

"I don't know. Rock climbing, sea kayaking, camping, that kind of outdoorsy stuff."

She wants to go camping … with me?

I suck in a shocked breath and choke on a piece of meat. She lifts an eyebrow as I cough.

"You know, there's this action called chewing. Might give that a try." Was that snark?

I force my lips not to grin and clear my throat. "Hmm. Never heard of it."

"You okay?" And there's the Rory I know. Always worried about others, even people she can't stand.

"Fine." I take a drink. "Your family's all into the outdoors. Why not just go with them?"

She sighs and pokes her food as her cheeks blush. "I need to be uncomfortable. I guess just getting out isn't enough."

I'm positive there's more to it than that. Might have something to do with her "hiking with some guy" comment this morning. Hadn't she said that her cousins and sister insisted she get out on the town, so to speak? What would her family think if that "some guy" is me?

"Okay. Adventure on the weekend. Workouts on weekday mornings. Deal?" I extend my hand across the table.

She swallows and gives me a firm nod. "Deal."

My hand tingles as it engulfs hers. She's trembling, all her bravado just a show. I drop her hand and scowl at the rest of my meal. If nothing else, by the time our deal's over, I'm going to make sure Aurora Wilde has more confidence in herself.

Chapter Fifteen

-Rory-

I pull open the gym door with more force than necessary, flinching as it hits the siding. After last night's meeting, I didn't sleep. Couldn't even attempt to sleep. No, I spent the night pacing and listing all the reasons this is a terrible idea.

Dax was horrible in school.

Patronizing with his nicknames and one-sided smiles.

He makes my sweat glands work overtime.

Then, my conscience would kick in, and I reminded myself of his better qualities.

Aside from calling me cupcake, he's been amicable.

He saved me from being eaten by the treadmill and didn't blow up when I kicked him you-know-where.

That pork he made last night was killer. If I hadn't been so nauseous with nerves, I would've scarfed the entire plate down and begged for seconds.

And last night, with those kids, he was amazing. Does

he really live by that motto they yelled? Integrity and honor always, no matter what, seems far different from the surly, quick to tease me boy I had to endure for ten years.

Aargh.

My nerves are shot.

Frazzled to the end of their existence.

And now I'm due for torture … er, training.

I weave my way to the open area where Dax balances on one foot. I think it's a tree pose or something. Dark circles puff under his eyes, too, and his hair sticks up wildly like he's been pulling on it. Maybe both of us aren't so keen with this idea.

"You ready?" Dax circles his hands high above his head, then to his side as he lowers his leg.

It's hard not to stare at the man with his defined muscles and his looming height that makes me, the second-tallest girl in our class, feel petite. But it's like studying one of Michelangelo's statues—emotionless. Purely educational.

Okay.

That's a lie.

I puff out my cheeks and toss my new bag toward the half-wall that divides the entry from the workout area. There're emotions, festering ones, too … like … like irritation, anger, hurt, but definitely not attraction.

Because that's impossible.

His eyes catch my T-shirt, causing him to smile. A swarm of mosquitos take flight in my stomach. Not the teeny kamikaze ones that dive in and out faster than you can see them. No, these are the large, slow variety that take their time pestering you before they suck your blood.

"First otters, now caribou?" He huffs a laugh and shakes his head.

I look down at my shirt with the caribou staring all wide-eyed and the words "You have how many books on your TBR?" circling him. I love him. He makes me laugh.

"I like making items for my readers." I point to all the merchandise he has displayed behind the counter. "It's not any different than your water bottles and muscle shirts." I shrug. "Except mine are clever, where yours … aren't."

I lift a shoulder, tip my head, and screw up my face in an apologetic expression. He bursts out laughing. Those pesky mosquitos in my gut turn to flipping, wing-buzzing giant dragonflies.

Oh, no.

This won't do.

I grit my teeth and squeeze what tummy muscles I have, willing my short-circuiting hormones to behave.

"All right, cupcake. Let's get to work."

The dragonflies burst into flames of fury. I narrow my eyes to slits and glare. He doesn't notice since he has turned to the window, but there's no way he doesn't feel my ire.

"We're going to take things easy the first few days, kind of work you into it." He motions me to stand next to him.

I copy him as he runs through a series of yoga poses. Each time we hold a new one, he explains the benefit of the position. At first, the benefits intrigue me, and I focus on my body, trying to picture how his words and what I'm feeling co-exist. Fascinating how they align in both my body and my brain.

By the end of the twenty minutes, I can care less about the merits of the stupid moves. My muscles are iron put in a forge, burning and losing all strength. My body trembles like an earthquake. And not the baby ones we get all the time. No, they shake like they're in a road-destroying, building-collapsing seism.

The infuriating part?

Dax isn't even fazed. It's like we haven't even been killing ourselves with yoga. He's not sweating, where my friendly caribou now clings to my chest like he's a baby monkey. Dax's muscles are steady, opposed to mine about to collapse and never work again. I understand that this is what he does for a living, but he should at least pretend to be winded.

"Good job, Wilde." He pats me on the shoulder, and my muscles give out, melting me into the padded floor. "Grab a drink. We're moving on from the fun stuff to work now."

"You have a messed-up sense of what's fun, Dax Payton," I wheeze out as I catch my breath.

"Come on." He reaches down a hand to help me up.

I want to slap it away, but I don't think I have the energy to stand, much less whack. My arm shakes as I lift it to him. I knew I wasn't in shape, but this is embarrassing.

He slides his hand in mine, then wraps his other around my elbow. Tingles race from the contact, making goosebumps erupt on my sweaty skin. He lifts me from the ground without effort. When my knees threaten to turn to liquid, his hand around my arm tightens to hold me upright. His thumb rubs the inside of my elbow. Rushing flames consume the goosebumps and burn my cheeks. I gulp, trying to find the energy to pull away but failing.

Without warning, he drops my arm and thumps me on the shoulder. "No more lazing about, cupcake. We've only got thirty more minutes left."

As we work through the rest of the time together, he doesn't touch me except a few times when he jerks my shoulders or feet into the position he wants. I'm totally okay with that fact. More than okay with it. It's obvious my body's in an overreactive state of existence at the moment.

Stress.

Has to be.

I knew it could tank your energy and health. I had no clue it could screw with your hormones. That's the only explanation for the tingles and the banked curiosity if it will happen again.

Chapter Sixteen

-Dax-

I pull up in front of Eagle's Nest Assisted Living, the house my mom lives in, and kill the engine. The place is cheery with its pale lemon-yellow paint, bright blue door, and flower beds bursting with color. Such a contrast to the poorly constructed cabin I grew up in that leaked cold air in more places than could be stuffed, even though each winter Mom and I would take old newspapers when Dad was gone and try. Before memories of that time can overwhelm me, I push open my truck door and saunter up the pathway.

Two men in their nineties sit on the porch playing checkers like they do each afternoon. Digger was an old gold miner from the Fortymile district and can tell the most amazing stories of his time scraping for riches. Virgil was a lawyer-turned-politician who fought for Alaska to become a state. Both are polar opposites in manner and history, and they can really get into it when they disagree on something. Yet, they've become tight friends living here.

"Who's winning today?" I ask as I rap on the screen door.

"I am," they both answer at the same time.

"Ha. You wish, poster boy," Digger wheezes, rubbing his hand over his grey beard that stretches down over his overalls.

"I don't wish. I know, you old gold bug." Virgil, with his clean-cut hair, snappy vest, and perfect bow tie, jumps two of Digger's pieces, then takes a long drink of his coffee.

"What?" Digger sputters, his eyes bugging from beneath his bushy eyebrows as he points his finger at the board, going back through the moves.

"I keep telling you to stay focused, but you insist on flirting with the new boarder through the window." Virgil shakes his head. "Remember that, young man. Letting a cute smile and baked goods distract you can only lead to failure."

My mind instantly races to Rory and the silky feel of her skin this morning. She'll never bring me baked goods and probably wouldn't even smile, but she most definitely has become a major distraction.

I clear my throat. "Duly noted."

"Ah, don't listen to the man, Dax." Digger waves his hand like he's swatting a fly. "A woman, especially one like my sweet Bessie had been—God rest her soul—is worth any loss their distraction brings. I would've let all the gold in the Fortymile flow through the sluice and right back into the creek if it meant I could spend my days with her. I'd rather be a poor man and have a life holding her, than keep my nose in the gold pan and strike it rich." He thumps his hand on the table, making the checker pieces jump. "As the Good Lord would have it, I got both."

He winks at me and smiles. I just chuckle and shake my head. Yet, his words burrow beneath my skin.

"Yeah, well … not everyone's as blessed as you." Virgil sets the game pieces back up.

"And whose fault's that?" Digger points his finger at Virgil. "When did you ever take the time to stop your pipe-laying politicking and actually listen? The way I see it from all your bellyaching of the past, you let your happily ever after slip through your fingers with your 'focus.'"

Watching the old man do air quotes almost makes me laugh.

"How you gather?" Virgil puffs up, clearly annoyed.

"You grouse about your Sylvia leaving you a week before your wedding, but do you realize you also brag about how much legislation and committees you spear-headed that same time. Now, I've done some prospecting—and as a gold miner, I'm mighty good at it—and I've got a theory. All that time you were making your mark as a statesman, did you ever listen to what she wanted? Did you ever take time to make her feel special or desired while you forged your place in Alaskan history? From the way you go on and on, I'd say the answer's no, and I'd have left you at the altar too."

"Dax, come on in," Nancy, the angel who owns and runs the facility, says from the other side of the screen, jerking my attention away from the argument. "How many times do I have to tell you that you don't need to knock, hun?"

"Probably a few more." I force a smile and wave at the men still arguing.

Digger's words circle in my head as the screen door screeches on its hinges, and I step inside. I want to bat them off as the mutterings of an old man, but they're spreading, laying a thick layer of doubt on my skin that makes me itch. Am I like Virgil, too focused on the outcome to see the good right in front of me?

"The new diet you suggested is helping your mom," Nancy says.

All thought pinpoints to this development.

"Really?"

"Yeah. She's remembering more and more each day. We aren't having to repeat things to her as much." Nancy pushes a hand through her salt and pepper hair. "It's really quite incredible. Just yesterday, she wanted her special meatloaf and told Rosie, our new boarder, the recipe from memory. Best meatloaf I've ever had."

I'd loved Mom's meatloaf growing up.

I blink away the moisture blurring my vision. The research on a high fat, moderate protein carnivore diet helping patients with impaired brain function had given me hope it could work for Mom. Nothing else had, so why not try? The fact that she showed improvement after only three weeks soared me higher than if I base-jumped off of Mount Denali.

"That's great," I choke out around the lump in my throat.

"Only downfall's now the other boarders want all meat, too, except when it comes to dessert … and potatoes." Nancy shakes her head. "They say they're supporting Jenny in her treatment, but aren't quite willing to go all in."

I glance at Nancy's bunched shoulders. She won't come out and say anything, but the added meat has to be hard on the expenses. She didn't convert her home into an assisted living to make bank, not with how little she charges for boarding. No, she does it to help others.

I hadn't considered the added expense the other boarders joining would cause. When I'd asked Nancy to try the new diet, I'd upped Mom's monthly payment to compensate. I'll have to swing by the bank and set up an anonymous monthly donation to the house. Nancy won't take it if I pay outright.

We step onto the back porch. My gaze zeroes in on Mom sitting on a loveseat in the sun. She's the same age as Nancy, in her late fifties. She should be in her own place, making her own meatloaf and planting her favorite flowers, not forced to live like a person forty years older. One night of my dad's rage going too far ripped what little freedom Mom had left away.

I rub the scar on my belly through my T-shirt. It's one of many. Mom has more. I shouldn't dwell on the should be's, not when it was a miracle we both survived. Not when there was hope Mom could improve more.

"Jenny, look who's here." Nancy pats me on the shoulder. "I'll bring you two out some coffee."

"Dax!"

Mom shifts in the loveseat to get up, so I quickly cross the porch and squeeze her into a bear hug. I lift her off her feet like I started doing when I outgrew her in eighth grade, and she squeezes me tight around the neck with a laugh. No matter how much she's lost, she always remembers this.

"Oh, I missed you." She pats me on the shoulder.

I set her back down in her spot and sit next to her. She clutches my hand, her smile trembling as she looks up at me. I shouldn't have stayed in the lower forty-eight as long as I did.

"I missed you too." I kiss her cheek. It's rosy for the first time in a long while. "You look good."

"I'm not sure where you found that info on the meat thing, but it's helping." Her eyes brighten, and I swallow the lump in my throat. "I'm remembering things, and not just to change out of my nightclothes before I come out of the bedroom." She laughs at herself, but it breaks my heart a little more. "Remember when we used to run out of food money each month and we'd have a week of peanut butter and pickle sandwiches? No matter what I did to make things stretch, that always ended up being what was left."

She *tsks* and shakes her head.

"I actually liked those sandwiches." I thread my hand through hers. I don't like talking about our past, but if she's excited to go down Memory Lane, I'll travel with her. I just need to keep us on the bright path and not veer into the dark.

"Really?" She looks up at me in surprise.

"At first, it was weird." I shrug. "But after the first or second one, I started looking forward to them."

I remember being glad the school served lunches, even if you couldn't afford them. Mom would have gone without the meager sandwiches, and I would've been embarrassed by them.

"Nancy says you gave away your secret meatloaf recipe." I bump her shoulder. "I thought you wanted to keep that in the family. You know, have the upper hand at potlucks and all."

"Pssh." She swats my arm. "This is family."

It's true. Nancy and the other boarders have become

more of a family to Mom than she's ever had before. I'm glad she has their love and support. She deserves it after what she went through with my dad … after I, in my selfish desire to be a normal teen, left her to face the monster alone.

Chapter Seventeen

-Rory-

A knock bangs on the door, exploding tiny bombs in my already throbbing head. I groan from my spot on the couch where I collapsed after attempting to get out of bed. Everything aches. My arms, my legs, even my eyelids hurt. I keep alternating between intense chills and burning heat. I'm emotional, lightheaded, nauseous, and can't think.

Basically, life sucks, and I want to die.

Whatever I caught shouldn't be spread to others. I pull the covers around me tighter, though social distancing's the last thing I want right now. A good hug would help, maybe some chicken noodle soup.

The obnoxious pounding bangs again, followed by five fast rings of the doorbell. What if there's a problem or a neighbor needs help? Well, they'll just have to get help somewhere else. I'm useless.

Only … my car's in the drive. They'll know I'm here. That I'm ignoring them.

"Grrr." I sit up, taking the blanket with me.

They'll know the instant they look at me that I'm on death's doorstep. Maybe *they'll* send help to me. Most of my neighbors know my mom. They could have her drop soup on the porch. In my muddled, non-functioning state, I've somehow lost my phone and haven't had the energy to look.

The thought of help coming gives me a boost of energy. I'll just stay well in my entryway, so I don't pass whatever this bug is along. Hiking the blanket up on my shoulders so I don't drop it, I swing the door open to Dax Payton on my porch.

I smirk as dark thoughts of payback niggle my mind.

"You look horrible." His eyebrows scrunch together.

That's it.

Social distancing's overrated.

I fist my hands in my blanket so I don't open the screen door and breathe on him. Even though he's a moose-sized jerk, I'd feel bad if he actually got sick.

"What are you doing here?" I lean against the door as fatigue settles back on me.

"You didn't answer my texts."

"Sorry. I can't find my phone." I close my eyes on my exhale but pop them right open. "How do you know where I live?"

"I saw you move in." He reaches for the door handle, his arms loaded down with grocery bags.

I step back as he lets himself in and walks past. "That was almost seven years ago."

"And?" He stops and rubs Chub's side with his foot.

Chub rolls on to his back, exposing his belly. It's the first he's moved since I relocated to the couch over an hour ago. Dax chuckles and gives in to the dog's request.

"What if I had moved?" I shut the door, flinching when it closes too hard.

My brain really hurts.

"You don't do change. You're predictable, like the tide." He scans me from head to toe as I rub my temple.

I hate that he's right. That everyone, my family, friends … even my nemesis, find me boring. I mean, I don't mind being reliable. It means people can count on me. Depend on me. But I'm tired of doing the expected.

I want to throw in an Arctic Ocean storm every now and then.

But not today.

Today, I want to curl up in my blanket and die.

Spontaneous will have to wait until after that.

"You should leave." I drag my feet to the closest place I can rest and sit on the end table. "You don't want to catch this."

I place my head in my hands and groan. Talking takes too much energy. I sniff as my nose tingles with threatening tears, then wrinkle my face in disgust. Great. Not only do I look like a grizzly coming out of hibernation, but I smell like one, too.

"Did you even read the information I gave you?" Dax's exasperation pulls my head up.

I shrug, and guilt adds its weight to my muscle aches. I meant to read it. Really, I did. After the first page expounding the benefits of being a Neanderthal with over ten research links of support including a detailing of how to track what I eat and a minuscule list of approved food, I tossed it on the corner of my desk in an overwhelmed panic.

"Could've saved you all of this." He motions up and

down with his hand at me, the grocery bags crinkling with the movement.

"*You* did this?" Of course, he's responsible for my misery. Hasn't that always been the case?

"No. You did this. Your body's addicted to carbs and sugar, you know, that stuff in your jumbo macchiato and head-sized cinnamon roll. Like any addict, you're having withdrawals."

"I'm not an addict, and I don't drink macchiatos."

He smirks.

Smirks!

Then turns to the kitchen.

"Don't get riled, Wilde. Pretty much all of America are addicts." He sets his bags on the island counter and starts unloading. "In fact, if sugar cane and coffee were discovered now instead of hundreds of years ago, they wouldn't have been approved for consumption. They're more like cocaine or heroin than food."

"Okay, fine. That's peachy." I cross to the island stools and plop down on one. "How do I fix the withdrawals and get you out of my house?"

His mouth twitches as he grabs a package of steaks, turns, and sets it next to the stove. I hate to admit this, but it's nice having him here. I'm that desperate for human interaction. At this point, I'd probably be good with anyone, even that horrid reviewer, if it meant I wasn't alone.

When he faces me, his expression's back to neutral. "I'll do as much as I can to help, but the best thing you can do is abstain and follow my clearly laid out instructions."

I groan and lay my head on my arms so I can rest and keep my eyes on him at the same time. "Just a tip. If you launch this program of yours, you might want to lead with 'Here's what to do when you're dying from detox' instead of boring your clients to death with research."

"Duly noted."

He opens and closes cabinets until he finds the cups. I don't even care that he's rummaging. If he's going to make the suffering stop, he can snoop all he wants. Well, in the kitchen, at least. If he steps a foot off the laminate wood flooring, I'll go all territorial grizzly on him, sick or not.

He scoops, pours, and mixes a concoction in water, adds ice, then sets it in front of me with a clunk on the granite. "Drink up, buttercup."

I sip and grimace. It's salty and disgusting. "What's this?"

"Electrolytes, exogenous ketones, and fat."

"Lovely." I take a bigger sip, not sure if my nauseous stomach will handle it.

If I throw up, I'm aiming for his mesh tennis shoes.

"Just sip on it and stop whining." He pulls coffee out of the bag and turns to the coffeemaker. "You'll start to feel better, I promise."

"Your promises don't mean much when I don't trust you."

I take another drink and cringe. Slimy ick coats my mouth, and it's not from the drink. Guilt tastes much worse than exonerated ketones.

"I'm sorry. That was rude." I lay my head back down and close my eyes.

"It's the truth."

"Doesn't mean I need to voice it."

His calloused fingers touch the top on my hand

where it sits on the counter before me, sending a shiver up my arm and down my back. My eyes pop open. His head hangs, and the muscle in his cheek pops like he gritted his teeth. He opens his mouth, then snaps it shut with a shake of his head.

"I'm going to make you a coffee you can drink, so pay attention, Wilde." His voice is gruff as he taps my fingers then jerks a grocery bag to him.

I watch as he pulls out a new kitchen gadget from his stuff and plugs it in. He searches through drawers, mumbling about my lack of organization until he finds a tablespoon. I should be paying attention to what he puts in my largest coffee mug and mixes with his wand blender thing, but I can't pull my gaze from his face.

Not once does he look directly at me. Just when I think he will, he jerks his attention somewhere else.

"Here." He sets the steaming, creamy mug in front of me. "Approved coffee."

"Thanks." I wrap my fingers around the hot mug and sip. It's not sweet, but, surprisingly, it's delicious. "Mmm. Yum."

He nods and turns to the stove. Still, he hasn't looked me in the eyes. For the first time in twenty years, I really wish he would.

Chapter Eighteen

-Dax-

I drum my fingers on the steering wheel to the beat of the music. It's cranked up high. Harder to talk when music blasts through the speakers. Easier to cover the awkward silence that's sure to be between Rory and I if I turn it down.

We've only been driving for thirty minutes, but already I regret picking camping as our first outing. After she recovered from the Keto Flu three days ago and asked what adventure we were doing first, I should've picked sea kayaking or hike to a glacier and ice climb. Both of those activities would have us home by evening.

Nope.

In my infinite wisdom, I decide to go all out and overnight.

Idiot.

My need to show her I'm going to hold up my side of the bargain will be the end of me. One torturous moment at a time. Her remark about not trusting me the other morning replays over and over again in my mind. With that alternating between the image of her wrapped adorably in the blanket at her front door glaring at me, it's a miracle I've been able to get anything done at all.

She turns the music down. "I never pegged you for a country fan."

"Hmm."

There's a lot she'd be surprised about me.

"Heavy metal, yes, especially with what you play in the gym."

"Those are video game soundtracks." I click on the blinker and turn onto the dirt road leading to the heart of the mountains.

"Really?" She turns in her seat, tucking her feet under her and leaning against the door.

The last thing I want is Rory Wilde's attention on me. Well, that's not true. I long for her to watch me, to notice that I'm no longer the punk kid who picked on her. But that longing won't help me stay focused on what's important.

Business.

Future.

Not the opinion of the woman who has hated me— for good reason—more than two-thirds of our lives.

"Yeah. Mostly it's the *Call of Duty* soundtracks." I slow over the ruts in the road, the truck leaning sideways on the rough road.

She untucks her feet and holds onto the door so hard her knuckles turn white. Does she think I'll wreck? Roll us over? I grit my teeth hard, making my temples hurt. So much for gaining her trust. This road's cake compared to the one we'll be on later.

"Why game soundtracks?" She squeaks out as a tire hits a rock and bounces the truck.

"Relax, Wilde. I've driven this road a hundred times."

"Sorry. It's not your driving." She loosens her grip but doesn't let go. "I just hate feeling like I'm going to tip."

"I promise. We won't tip."

"Okay."

"The whole point of this deal is to get you out of your comfort zone, not scare you." I should tone down the annoyance, but its either that or I do what I want to do and slide my hand into hers to help comfort her.

The second won't do, so annoyance it is.

"I'm not scared." She actually sounds indignant.

I stare at her, one doubting eyebrow raised.

She shifts and crosses her arms. "Okay. Maybe a little."

I scoff and shake my head, turning my attention back to the road. It smoothes back out to normal ruts and bumps, and Rory relaxes even more. If I distract her, maybe she'll relax all the way.

"They're designed to amp up the adrenaline." I lean to the side and rest my elbow on the armrest.

"I'm sorry, but what the heck are you talking about?" Rory scrunches her forehead and pushes her glasses up.

"The soundtracks for the games. They compose them to increase the intensity of the player's visceral connection to the game."

I point to a porcupine clinging to a tree. She gasps in delight beside me, so I stop and roll down her window. As she snaps pictures with her phone, I can't pull my eyes from her. She has a bandana tied around her head to hold her hair out of her face. It exposes the slender slope of her neck where it connects to her jaw and tempts me to lean over and—

"Thanks for stopping." She smiles at me, and I jerk my attention forward and nod. "So, you picked the music on purpose, like tapping into the subconscious warrior or something?"

I shrug. "Yeah."

My throat's dry from just how much I want to give into temptation. It's like I'm back in high school, leaning over her desk just so I can inhale her essence. I'm on more than dangerous ground. It's a mine-riddled battle-field. One wrong step and all my goals are destroyed.

"That's brilliant." Her compliment, the first one I've gotten since third grade, doesn't help my struggle.

My hands sweat—shoot, my entire body feels drenched. I open my window and lean my arm on it to get a breeze up my sleeve. Maybe by the time we stop, I'll be dried out some.

"It's helped me." She gives me a small, shy smile, and my gaze glues to it, branding the slight lift of her lips in my brain. "I fly through typing words when I'm there."

"Good."

The truck hits a rut and lurches to the side. I twist the volume up and force my attention back on the road. "Burning Man" by Dierks Bentley plays, taunting me to remember who I am and why it'll never work with Rory. I sing along, focusing on the words and ignoring her. Because, the truth of the matter is, I'm probably more burning man than not, and she's always been one hundred percent angel.

Chapter Nineteen

-Rory-

The wind howls and the sides of the tent flap in a violent cacophony. I pull my sleeping bag tighter around me where I sit in the middle of my tent, lean my forehead on my knees, and squeeze my eyes shut. Why did I ever agree to come camping of all things?

Sure, the mountain drive was beautiful, and I enjoyed the moose tenderloin Dax roasted over the fire, even if he didn't bring s'mores or potato salad. But the minute the wind had picked up and dark clouds had built on the horizon, I knew we should've packed up our camp on the freaking cliff and gone home.

Okay, it's not a cliff, per se. But it might as well be with how the mountain meadow slopes to the rocky edge we're supposed to climb tomorrow. He's practically popped our tents in a potential flood zone.

"No. He knows what he's doing. You're just freaking out."

Talking to myself doesn't help when the whipping of thin tent nylon drums all around me. Plus, it's dark, and

I can't see. I didn't pack a lantern since it's summer in the land of the Midnight Sun. I dart my eyes around, hoping for a hint of light. It's not supposed to get dark in Alaska during the summer, which means those sinister clouds press down on us, encasing us in stormy gloom.

I hate the dark.

And nature.

Thunder cracks, and a flash of lightning brightens the tent. I bite my lip to keep from crying out. Suddenly, rain pelts the fabric. This isn't a gentle tapping, it's a downright barrage. The earth booms, followed quickly by another flash of light.

I can't help it.

I scream.

And not just a shriek of surprise. Nope. This is an all-out, Jason with his mask and chainsaw just showed up behind me scream of utter terror.

The tent zipper yanks open, and Dax climbs in, bringing the blessing of his flashlight with him. All he has on are athletic shorts hanging low on his hips, which is ridiculous since its absolutely freezing up here. Rivulets of water stream from his hair down his muscled chest, but even that sight doesn't pull me out of my terror.

"What's wrong? Are you okay?" He wipes the water from his face and scans the tent.

It's obvious from his groggy expression I've woken him from a deep sleep. I have no clue how he got to me as fast as he did, but the fact that he rushed over sparks a small ember in my gut that maybe everything will be okay.

The storm cracks another death bolt, dousing the ember. I cut off my shriek by covering my mouth with my hand. Dax's fully awake now, his expression softening as he finally really looks at me.

"Hey." He places his hand on my knee. "It's just a little mountain storm. It'll blow over as fast as it came."

I shake my head as all the possibilities of disaster flip through my head. As a romantic suspense author, I've done a lot of research and have a ton of catastrophes catalogued. There are so many things that could go wrong.

"Seriously, practically every time I come here, one of these blows in." He runs his hand through his hair, flinging water.

"No ... it's just ... I can't." I tangle my fingers further into my sleeping bag fabric.

Dax studies me. My stomach twists with the scrutiny. A gust hits the fabric, and I dart my eyes to the tent seams that will surely rip apart at any moment.

"Why are you so afraid?" He whispers the question into the violent din, but I still hear him.

"Are you kidding me?" My voice comes out a panicked screech that I can't control. "What if lightning strikes the tent and incinerates me? Or worse, what if a flash flood races down this meadow of yours and washes us over the cliff? Or the rain loosens the ground and the rocks holding this piddly stretch of grass gives way and we fall down the mountainside in a rockslide buried forever?"

"Rory." He squeezes my knee, but my words are a steam engine barreling out.

"The world's just waiting to rip us to shreds, and you've plopped us here on a nice, grass-filled platter."

"It's going to be okay." He shifts closer, putting his hand on my shoulder. "I promise."

My chin trembles, and tears chill my cheeks. "It wasn't okay for Sadie or Melinda when the avalanche hit. They had no warning, Dax. No clue the world was about to swallow them whole."

"I remember." He brushes his thumb against my cheek.

I latch onto his arm, needing something solid to hold onto before I blow away in the chaos around me.

"Melinda died, suffocating in a tomb of snow, and Sadie's body was so burned from being pushed against the cabin's wood stove that she almost died too." The horror of it all—of watching Sadie's months of agonizing recovery and knowing they had no way to predict the avalanche would happen—planted so firmly in my brain that for almost an entire year every time I stepped outside I almost passed out from fear.

"I remember you spent a lot of time in the library that year." He places his hand on mine still in a death grip on his bicep. "Well, a lot more than normal."

"You do?"

"Yeah. I'm sorry you had to go through that."

"It got better. I don't mind the outdoors now." I peel my fingers from the bag and flex them in my lap. "But this … this is too much."

"I'm sorry, Rory. I didn't know."

"How could you? We haven't spoken this much since third grade." I try to laugh it off, but it comes out more a teary gurgle than laughter.

"I can take you home." He sits back on his heels. "It won't be a fun drive in this storm, but if we take it slow, we should be fine."

I shake my head and squeeze my eyes closed. The thought of failing—of giving in to this fear and giving up—chills me more than the crisp mountain air. I don't want to chicken out, to let the apprehension of possibilities keep me from experiencing more than just my small, safe world in the Seward city limits.

"You've been through storms like this and promise we won't get washed off the edge." My voice cracks.

"I promise."

Those two words let me take a deeper breath.

"I want to stay." I force my fingers to flex.

"Okay." He nods, pride in his eyes as he looks at me.

I huff out another breath and sit a little taller.

"Would it help if I sleep in here?" He peers around the space. "It's big enough for both of us."

The thought of being cozy in the small tent warms my cheeks, but not enough to push my anxiety away.

"Can we—" This is going to sound ridiculous. I should just suck it up and stay in the tent.

"What, Rory?" His voice is gentle and not at all condescending.

"Can we sleep in the truck? I think I'd feel safer there, less chance of being swept off the cliff."

"Yeah." He nods without hesitation. "We can do that."

He helps me get my cheap rain poncho on and hands me my shoes. Only then do I realize his feet are bare and muddy. Probably freezing too. He doesn't give me any time to comment on it though since he wads my sleeping bag under one arm and unzips the flap with the other.

"Ready to run?" he asks as he hands me the flashlight.

When I nod, he steps out of the tent. Instead of dashing for the truck, he reaches his empty hand in for me. Only when I'm standing does he take off, keeping my hand in his until we reach the truck. Three minutes later, he's climbing into the driver's seat, fully clothed and in his sweatshirt. He cranks the key and turns the heat to high, then leans the seat back. I do the same and lay on my side facing him.

"Oh, yeah. Much more comfortable than my pad and sleeping bag." He winks at me, then turns serious. "You better?"

"Yep."

Lightning chooses that moment to crack the clouds open. I flinch and tremble despite the warm air coming from the vents. Dax's hand stretches toward me, slow, like he's not sure if I'll pull away. It may be stupid, but I don't want to pull away.

His fingers slide along my palm, then fold around my hand in a comforting embrace. He swallows, then closes his eyes. His thumb rubs a soothing path along the back of my hand, sending tingles up my arm and down my spine. As I stare at his face, my eyelids grow heavy, and, though the storm still beats against the truck, my fear slowly inches out like the tide.

Chapter Twenty

-Dax-

Soft, warm fingers wrap around my palm. I open my eyes, surprised to still find Rory's hand in mine. The fact that she let me take it at all had me lying awake most of the night, convincing myself it didn't mean anything.

She was scared, and I was here.

That's it.

But watching her flinch in her sleep each time the thunder crashed and seeing her relax with just a stroke of my thumb across the back of her hand had me wide awake. Well, that and the fact that a man measuring almost six-six isn't meant to sleep in a driver's seat. I roll my cramped neck and ease my hand from Rory's.

If I don't get out of here, my back will permanently be crooked. And I'll probably lean over and kiss Rory awake. Neither would be good … well, good for my future.

Slowly, so I don't wake her, I pull the handle and open the door. I need to get breakfast cooking, so we can climb some rocks and go home. Overnighting's a mistake I won't make again on these little adventures of hers. There are a ton of experiences I can give her that won't end up with her sleeping next to me, tempting me.

I pull the tarp off the camp stove and find the sausage in the cooler. It's sizzling and filling the crisp morning air with its spices when Rory finally climbs out of the truck. When my eyes instantly snap to her, I groan and clench my teeth to keep my mouth from gaping.

She's found my spare sweatshirt in the back seat and swims in it. Her hair's messy, completely opposite of its normal, perfect style. She shivers, then yawns, covering her mouth with her hand engulfed in my sleeve.

Forget tempting.

She's downright bewitching.

Casting her captivating spells to lure me into my doom.

"I hope you don't mind." She pulls at the front of the sweatshirt. "I forgot to grab my jacket last night."

"It's fine."

Just peachy.

I'll have to burn it so I don't obsess over her lingering presence. Turn the stupid shirt into a security blanket or something. Darn shame. I liked that shirt.

I clear my throat and turn back to the food. "Breakfast'll be done in ten. I'd like to break camp so we can head out as soon as we finish climbing."

"Oh. Okay." Her soft answer laced with disappointment drags my gaze to her.

She's fiddling with the cuff, staring at it like it holds the secrets to life. Her cheeks pink. Probably just the chilly morning air. Then her ears redden, and my heart races in my chest. Rory's blushing ... because of me?

Did she feel the electricity coursing through the truck last night too? It wasn't the lightning. No, it was an entrancing connection zinging between us. I'm sure.

"Thanks for understanding last night and not laughing." She swallows and looks up at me. "I didn't think I'd react so strongly to the storm."

The zing fizzles to a lump of dejection in my gut. Of course, she's embarrassed by her freak out. My head needs a few good bumps on the pitch if I'm this disappointed in her reaction to last night. Maybe a kick or two for good measure.

Rory has and will always see me as the kid who terrorized her growing up. There's nothing I can do to change that.

"No problem." I shrug off the confusion and distraction she creates and focus on what's important—completing this outing so I hold up my end of the bargain. "I'm going to check the rocks while this finishes cooking."

I stride away toward the drop off. Hopefully, by the time I get back she'll be out of my clothes and my brain can think straight. I breathe in the chilly air still laced with rain and wet grass. I stop on the edge of the rocks, close my eyes, and take another cleansing inhale.

Focus.

Future.

I envision my gyms filled with people excited about getting healthy. It's fuzzy, but if I just sharpen my dream a little more, I'll picture it. I shift through hazy images of people I've helped in the past. Their thrilled expressions when they reach their goal warm me from the inside, pushing the morning chill away.

The images slip from one to another until they zero

in on Rory trembling as she holds a yoga position. Rory struggling to lift herself on the pull up bar, whooping when she finally makes it. Rory sighing next to me in the darkened cab of the truck, relaxing to my touch even though the storm still rages.

I curse low and jerk my eyes open. Rubbing my hand over my racing heart, I remind myself of my dreams and goals. There's no room in them for Rory Wilde. Even if there is, I doubt she'd be interested.

Chapter Twenty-One

-Rory-

I lower myself into the almost scorching water of my hot tub, hissing as my skin complains. After the confusing weekend and two days of awkward workouts with Dax, I need this. I wince at the heat and glance around the tub as my sister and cousins make similar noises.

"Dang, Rory, do you have to set it to boiling?" Emmy's down for the celebratory picnic the family's having tomorrow for Violet and Kemp.

They're back from winning the Race Across the Americas.

"It's healing," I counter with a whistle.

"If my skin blisters, I'm not going to be happy." Violet cringes.

"It's not that bad." Denali looks like she's about to throw up from the heat.

"Oh, for goodness sake." Sadie stomps over to the garden hose, cranks it on, and plops the end into the tub.

Cold water rushes past my legs, quickly gobbled up by the heat. We all sigh in unison, then bust up laughing. My eyes bounce to each of them, filling me with an effervescent happiness I've missed by keeping weighty secrets from them.

"So … how's married life?" I ask Violet.

We haven't had much time to talk since they got back a few days ago. All the family had worried she was making a huge mistake pretending to be engaged. If things had gone wrong, her ability to never forget her life's events would make her replay the disappointment over and over again. Then, when she and Kemp got married in Vegas, I thought for sure Uncle Will would lose it. Even though I write romance and make money off of happily-ever-afters, I didn't think it would work between them.

Her face radiates as she smiles and closes her eyes. "It's amazing."

She sighs, and a twinge of jealousy tweaks my heart. I should be thrilled, not envious. Sadie splashes water at Violet, causing her to sputter.

"I still can't believe you got married in Vegas." Sadie splashes Violet again. "Without your family, especially me, your loving sister."

With each of the last three words, Sadie splashes more water over Violet's head for emphasis. I bite my lip, tucking away bits of conversation to use in a future book. Fake relationships sell, and Violet and Kemp's was epic.

"I'm sorry, okay?" Violet holds up her hands in surrender.

"Not okay." Sadie crosses her arms in a mock pout, but she can't hold it long before a smile breaks free.

"Totally okay. Bjørn and I were at Mom and Dad's when you two got hitched. I swear Dad's vein almost popped out of his head. He even asked Bjørn how long it would take the helicopter to make it to Nevada."

"I do feel bad about that." Violet cringes. "I mean, not bad that we got married like we did. I loved our wedding, but making Dad upset sucks. Mom wants to have a big reception, so I'm going to be calling on all you guys to help."

"Absolutely." Denali drapes her arm over Violet's shoulder for a side hug. "Anything for the first of us to get hitched."

"Shocked the heck out of me." Violet shakes her head and motions to me. "I know friends to lovers is like a thing in romance, but I honestly hadn't ever considered it."

"Those make the best stories." I wag my eyebrows at her. "Especially when *both* the hero and heroine get hit with the unexpected love bug between the eyes."

"We definitely got hit." Violet shakes her head. "Bulldozed, more like it."

"Speaking of writing, how's the adventure experiment going?" Emmy turns to me, and I wish I would've just kept my big mouth shut.

"Fine." I skim my hands across the top of the water.

"Experiment? What experiment?" Violet sits up straight.

"She's having trouble finding her muse, so we told her she had to change things up." Sadie hops out of the hot tub and turns off the hose.

"First, she went to the gym, but that didn't seem to be enough." Emmy shrugged. "You'd think a room full of men showing off their muscles would rev up the ol' brain."

"My brain isn't old," I scoff.

"I don't know." Emmy tips her head to the side, examining me. "All your fretting probably aged it at least ten or twenty years."

"Whatever." I roll my eyes, though she may have a point.

"We flew with Dax on our way out for the race. It seems like he's grown out of his obnoxiousness." Violet scrunched up her face. "In fact, Kemp hit it off with him. They've been texting back and forth about snowboarding like a couple of long-lost friends."

"Yeah. Dax's fine."

I downplay just how fine he is. No use giving them more than absolutely necessary. They'll jump on any hint I might not find Dax vile like a pack of starving wolves.

"He's better than fine." Violet waves herself off. "He's smoking hot."

"Really?" Emmy turns a conniving grin to me.

"What?"

"Oh, nothing." She focuses back on Violet. "So, when the room full of muscled guys didn't work, we told Rory she had to go on adventures or find a guy to date and that it couldn't be Mark or tagging along with any of you disgustingly sweet couples."

"Yeah. He's too safe." Violet nodded. "Have you gone out yet?"

My heart hammers in my chest as I stare at the water. I really don't want to tell them. I also don't want to pile any more secrets between us. I swallow and nod. Squealing snaps my eyes up to their giddy faces.

"I knew something had happened. You've had this look on your face all day." Emmy circles her finger at my face.

"Have not," I scoff.

"What'd you do?" Sadie asks.

"Just went camping and rock climbing." I shrug like it's no big deal.

"You went camping *and* rock climbing?" Denali eyes widen, "Like, in the mountains and everything?"

"Of course, in the mountains." I pull on the end of my hair.

"Did you share a tent?" Violet wags her eyebrows.

"No. I borrowed yours since—"

"Wait a second. Who gives a rip about where you slept or what you did!" Emmy leans forward and spears me with a gaze I know I won't be able to dodge. "Who did you go with?"

Every eye turns to me as an unnatural stillness settles over us. Between the heat of the hot tub and my heart banging against my chest, trying to escape, I might just pass out. I open my mouth to tell them, but nothing comes out. Each second that passes, Emmy's face morphs further into glee. I clear my throat and try again.

"Dax."

"Dax Payton?" Denali looks horrified.

Emmy does a little dance. "Oh, I knew this would be good."

"He's really not that bad." Violet pats Denali's shoulder.

"Not that bad?" Denali swings her arm to me, almost hitting my face. "He terrorized her growing up."

I tip my head back and forth, weighing her words and scrunching my face. "Terrorize is a bit harsh."

"Really?" Denali crosses her arms.

"I mean, he called me names, but that was all."

Why am I defending him? Doesn't he still call me names? Cupcake has never been my moniker.

"I don't believe this." Denali throws her hands wide, and Sadie and Violet dart amused glances at each other.

"Oh, this is so much better than just finding a man to take you on a date." Emmy's practically panting with delight.

"How's that?" I might need a drink.

Or better yet, maybe I'll take Chub, get in the car, and drive to the Yukon for an extended trip. In fact, relocating might be the best possibility.

"You're sleeping with the enemy." Emmy rubs her hands together.

"I'm not sleeping with anyone!" I shout, splashing her as the other three turn their shocked expressions to me.

"It's a figure of speech." Emmy sputters. "Geesh. You'd think, as a writer, you'd know that."

"Horrible idiom," I shoot back.

Violet gasps.

"What did you just call me?" Emmy points to herself.

"Idiom, like phrase, not idiot." Sadie pats Emmy on the shoulder.

"Whatever." Emmy waves it off, already moving on from the supposed offense like she bounces through life. "It's not important. What's important is the fact that Rory's camping with a smoking hottie who also happens to be the man she's loathed for decades."

"That's stretching it a little." I put my index and thumb up in front of my face, measuring an inch.

"It's like the perfect plot for one of your romance novels," Violet injects.

"Except there's no romance going on," I point out.

"But you want there to be," Emmy counters. "I can see it on your face."

"There's nothing on my face."

"Oh, yes, there is." Emmy needs to go back up whatever mountain she came off of. "There's doubt and gnawing of your lip and staring off into the distance. It's all there."

"You know, she has been pretty distracted lately," Denali adds.

"I have not." This is getting out of control.

"Yeah, you have." Sadie pats my shoulder, but I smack her hand away. "The other day, I watched you wash a spoon for an entire three minutes. I figured you were working out a story plot or something, but usually when you're doing that, you pace your office or bang your head on your desk."

"You guys are crazy." I shift uncomfortably in my seat.

"Has he kissed you?" Emmy asks.

"What? No!" I furrow my eyebrows, as my stomach clenches.

"But you want him to," Emmy insists, and I'm really thinking I need to switch my favorite cousin to either Violet or Sadie.

Neither of them are this overbearing.

Or insightful.

I shake my head and climb out of the hot tub. "I'm going to go get us drinks."

There's no way I'm disappointed he hasn't kissed me. Even if I was, it wouldn't do me any good. Dax Payton has never had any interest in me, and probably never will.

Chapter Twenty-Two

-Dax-

I pull up to Violet Wilde's parents' house, put the truck in park, and stare at the two-story log cabin with balloons floating on the privacy fence. My thumb taps a spastic beat on the steering wheel as sweat pools in my pits. I haven't been this nervous since I interviewed with the head coach of the Hurricane pro rugby team my senior year.

If I leave now, just put the truck in drive and go, no one will know I was ever here. I reach for the keys, my hand shaking. I jerk the keys out of the ignition, angry at my hesitation.

At my fear.

I told Kemp I would stop by, so I'm staying. Being a man of my word, not some cop-out. I roll my shoulders and stalk to the sign on the fence pointing to the gate.

As soon as I can see over the cedar planks, my gaze zeroes in on Rory like a heat-seeking missile. She's sitting off to the side, kind of looking glum. What could be getting her down at such a happy celebration? Did she get another bad review?

Mark walks up to her, hands her a plate, and sits down next to her. Burning pain stabs my gut and singes up my throat. Everything in me wants to break down the fence, rush over to Rory, scoop her in my arms, and growl at Mark that she's mine. This green monster has bit at my stomach and raged in my mind ever since high school.

I figured, one day, Mark would grow a backbone and tell her how he feels. After all these years, he hasn't, and I'm still stuck watching from the sides, hating his guts for being so close to her.

Except, I'm not really on the sideline anymore, am I?

No. She chose *me* to take her on her adventures.

Not Mark.

A sense of victory cools the raging jealousy, and a satisfied smirk lifts the side of my mouth. It settles further as she pushes around the food on her plate. She doesn't do that to the food I make her. She gobbles down whatever I cook, making small comments of delight.

I open the gate and pretend to scan the guests. No use announcing that I'm obsessed with Rory. At least not yet.

When I let my eyes connect with hers, she stiffens and holds her breath. Has she not told Mark about our arrangement? My gaze flicks to Mark, thrilled that she's keeping things from him.

Keeping *me* from him.

I saunter over. Mark's brought her a plate full of off-limit junk. I pointedly look at her plate, then raise my eyebrow at her in challenge. She glares, though her cheeks pink, and a thrill of excitement rushes up my spine.

"See you at the gym tomorrow?" I can't help myself, and the way Mark freezes next to her seals the petty victory.

"Maybe," she snaps back, but there's no bite to it.

I just chuckle and shake my head. If I don't walk away, I'll push her too far. Be even more of the jerk I've always been.

Hard to woo someone when they hate you.

Icy reality hits me like a spring torrential rain. Rory isn't part of my five-year plan. Wasn't even a possibility a few weeks ago. Yet, if I can win Rory's heart *and* build an empire, life'll be perfect.

I turn and head toward Kemp before I do something stupid and blow any chance I have with her. The way Mark scorches me with his look, it wouldn't take much to spark the fuse and make him explode. Beating her best friend to a pulp wouldn't make a good impression—with her or her parents.

When I get to the newlyweds, Violet pulls me into a hug. "I'm so glad you're here."

Nice. I have one cousin already won over. That leaves, what, two more and a sister? Not to mention the parents.

"Congratulations, guys." I reach out my hand to Kemp.

He takes it and yanks my arm into a bro hug. "Thanks."

"Your race was pretty epic." I clap him on the shoulder. "The Andes' slopes as gnarly as they look?"

"They've got bite." Kemp drapes his arm across Violet's shoulders and kisses her temple.

Her cheeks have gone pale. With how she can't forget things, maybe bringing the snowboarding part up wasn't the best idea. I don't want her reliving the avalanche during her party.

"So, Vi, were those women in Vegas as crazy as they seemed?"

I'm hoping the question will make her think of something happy. It'd be horrible having the condition she does. If I had to relive my childhood through perfectly remembered videos in my head, I probably wouldn't be on this earth long.

"Oh, my goodness. They're the best." She smiles, and her eyes instantly light up.

Kemp catches my eye and nods a thanks. Warmth spreads through my chest. I nod back and listen to Violet as she gushes about the four fairy godmothers who helped make her and Kemp's wedding perfect.

"Well, look who it is." Another of Rory's cousins walk up.

She was two years behind us in school and moved to town in high school, so I can't remember her name. I do remember her being kind of wild, always getting in trouble for doing crazy stunts.

"Emmy Glenn, just in case you forgot." She sticks her hand out, her handshake firm.

"It's been awhile." I get an itch between my shoulder blades as she gives me a quick scan.

"So, how's the gym business? Quite the *adventure* you've got going on there." She smirks and one eyebrow raises.

Violet elbows Emmy. She looks at her cousin and

shrugs. These two definitely know that I'm helping Rory, but do they know she's helping me?

"It's going good." I put my hands in my pockets. "Can't complain."

"Oh, I bet you can't." Her sassy tone has my ears itching.

Just what has Rory been telling them?

My phone beeps. I pull it out of my pocket and groan when I read Vince's name on the text.

"Excuse me. I need to take care of this. Congratulations, guys." I smile at the three of them and walk to a high table set up for dirty dishes. No one's there at the moment.

Vince: How's the test run going? We're anxious to hear.

Me: Fine. Just like I expected.

Vince: Can you get results sent to us to look over?

I clench my teeth. I never said I'd send them updates. Getting someone to peak health isn't a gradual climb you can always progress. Sometimes, it'll seem like the lifestyle change isn't working, then, suddenly, the body awakens and takes off. Vince's oblivious to anything but money.

Me: Yes, at the end of the three months.

Vince: I'd like something in two weeks. Send it to my assistant. Also, up your social media game like we talked about. You're still nowhere. We need you out there.

I don't respond, just lock my screen and shove the phone in my pocket. I turn just in time to see Rory approaching. She's trying to appear casual, but her eyes keep darting to Emmy and Violet whispering on the other side of the yard.

She sets her still full plate on the table. She picks at chipping paint on the edge of the top, then pulls on the hem of her shirt. Her teeth bite her lip, pulling my attention to her very kissable mouth. That's her sign she's nervous, has been since elementary school. But nervous about what?

She darts a glance over to her cousins and huff. "What did Emmy say to you?"

I stifle my smile and shrug. "She just asked how the gym business was going."

"Really?" Her shocked face finally turns to me.

"Yeah."

Her shoulders relax, and she mutters, "Stupid paranoia."

I scan the yard to keep my expression neutral.

"I thought there'd be more people here to celebrate." It only looks like family's present.

"This is just for family and close friends. We'll have a bigger reception later."

My heart sinks. I'm neither of those.

"I probably should head out then." I take a step backward toward the gate.

She touches my arm, and I freeze. The contact's soft

and quick, like a butterfly landing and taking off, but my skin tingles. Her cheeks pink again as she pushes up her glasses.

"If Kemp invited you, then you're supposed to be here." She looks at her plate, and her cheeks go from pink to red. "I'm sorry about the food. Mark got my plate. He must've forgotten."

Yeah, right. That man remembers everything Rory says and does. More than likely, he picked the food he did because he doesn't like things changing between them, even something as little as food.

"Did you say anything to him about it?" I ask, hoping she stuck up for herself.

"No, I—" She cuts herself off.

So, I finish for her. "Didn't want to hurt his feelings."

She shakes her head and looks at the ground. "That easy to read, huh?"

"You've always been thoughtful of others. Always. I just don't think you've ever thought of yourself."

She blinks up at me, her mouth in a slight O. She looks so darn cute I want to wrap her in my arms and tell her all the amazing qualities she has. My phone beeps again, then again, pulling me back to reality. I pull my phone out of my pocket enough to peek at the screen. It's just Tony, but the ASAP on the front of the text means I shouldn't ignore it.

"Looks like I need to head out." I shove the phone back down.

What I'd like to do is stay and see just how long Rory'll stand here with me. See if she'd introduce me to her family and pull me into the tight fold happening here. The only place I've ever had that was on the rugby pitch. Since my business exploded, even that's started to disappear.

"Oh. Okay." Her disappoint kicks my heart rate up one hundred percent.

"Listen. If you want to eat the fried fish or the potato salad, do it." I take a step closer. "But make that choice because it's what *you* want. Not because you think I'll be disappointed or because you don't want to hurt Mark's feelings. It doesn't matter what either of us thinks." I step even closer and drop my voice. "You're so much stronger than you give yourself credit for, Aurora Wilde. I just wish you'd see it like I do."

Her chest heaves as she stares up at me. It'd be so easy to close the last foot separating us, but if I'm going to finally kiss Rory, it's not going to be in front of her entire family.

I reach past her so her heat pushes against me. She sucks in a breath and holds it while I snag a piece of fish from her plate. As I pull back, I lean in and whisper against her ear.

"See you in the morning, cupcake." Popping the fish in my mouth, I give her a wink and step backward.

When I turn toward the gate, I spy Mark fuming. I stifle the urge to smile in victory at him. It's better to just pretend I don't see him so he doesn't do something crazy, like finally ask Rory to marry him.

The thought turns the tasty halibut to ash in my mouth. I should have kept my distance. If Mark thinks I'm a threat to him someday getting Rory, he might finally grow that backbone. Knowing Rory and how much she hates conflict, she might just say yes.

Chapter Twenty-Three

-Rory-

As I walk the sidewalk to the gym, I type notes in my phone for my book. I woke up in the middle of the night with all kinds of ideas of how to fix the plot bombarding me. For the first time in months, I'm excited about the story, which meant I hardly slept.

But who can sleep when your muse finally pops up carrying goodies?

A low chuffing sound freezes my steps and snaps my attention up. A black bear stares me down not fifteen feet from me. It's leaning from one side to the next like it's sizing me up.

"Hey, bear. Go on." My voice cracks, not showing the strength I need to portray to get it to move on.

It chuffs again, this low mix between a growl and a huff, and takes a step forward. My skin chills. Being mauled by a bear would not help my looming deadline any.

"Come on, bear, get," I yell louder and wave my hands up.

It pushes on its hind legs and opens its mouth so I can see all its teeth. I take a step back but stop myself from fleeing. Bears love to chase, and I'm not that fast.

"Hey! Hey!" I wave my hands, but it doesn't stop it from taking four more steps toward me.

A blaring of an air horn surprises me, making me scream. It also startles the bear. Its furry hind end would be cute as it rushed away if I wasn't so terrified.

Dax stalks up to me, his nostrils flaring. I step back, not sure why he's angry. His arm gestures wildly toward where the bear was.

"What were you thinking letting him get so close?" His loud voice blasts out, making me feel like a child.

"I wasn't paying attention." I shove the phone into my bag and hold it close to my body to stop my shaking.

He mutters something too low for me to hear and pushes a trembling hand through his hair. He's not angry. Dax Payton's scared … for me. My mouth goes dry and my heart picks up for a completely different reason.

He glances to where the bear went then spears me with a gaze full of worry and concern. "You okay?"

I nod, not able to find my voice.

"You sure?" He lifts his hand to me but drops it to his side.

"Yeah."

All I got is a whisper as disappointment fills my throat. I want him to step closer. Want him to wrap me in his arms and hold me until I'm done quaking. Never in my wildest dreams would I have thought I'd feel safe with Dax, but I do.

"Let's get to it then." He turns to the door and

stomps off. "I sure hope you pay more attention tonight on our adventure."

The annoyance is back in his voice, but I'm on to him. His attitude doesn't fool me anymore.

"What are we doing this time?" I walk past as he holds the door open for me.

I step closer than necessary just to see how he reacts. He doesn't. Maybe his concern's just for someone's safety, like a hero complex.

Or insurance.

Can someone sue a business if a bear attacks on their property?

Once again, I've imagined more to the situation than there really is. That's the problem with only living in my head and rarely getting outside of my comfort zone. I've forgotten how to read people.

"The salmon are running, and I've a tournament this weekend, so I hope it's okay that we do our adventure a few days early. I'll pick you up at eleven for shore fishing. We'll park over by your sister's boyfriend's place and walk in."

"We're staying in town?" My fingers tingle.

Doesn't that negate our deal being secret?

"Is that a problem?" When he asks, he's so close behind me his breath brushes against my neck.

I stop and look over my shoulder. "No."

One side of his lip twitches up slightly before his face becomes a mask of indifference.

"Good." His pat on my shoulder's one he'd give a teammate or one of the kids he coaches. "You've wasted enough time making faces at the bear. Let's get to work."

I put my stuff against the half wall that divides the entrance from the workout area, trying to sort out what just happened. For the next hour I work hard, pushing myself to my limits, more so I can keep my brain from flipping over what just happened. It didn't help.

By the time the workout's done, both my muscles and my head hurt. Dax, on the other hand, isn't even affected by our earlier exchange, which has me concluding his concern and worry was more because he's a decent person who doesn't want someone—anyone—to end up a bear's breakfast.

"Your muscles are getting stronger, Wilde."

He lifts a free weight from the floor and puts it away. His words, like what he'd say to a teammate, confirm my conclusion. I guess teammate's better than enemy. It's a maneuvering toward possible friendship. The praise makes the soreness worth it, even if I'd rather he punctuate it with a kiss instead of a proverbial fist bump.

"You did good today, cupcake."

Dax's nickname shatters my rising jubilation at the compliment.

"I wish you wouldn't call me that. It makes me think of muffins and muffin tops." The words are out of my mouth before I can check them.

I pull at my sweaty shirt just to make sure it's not clinging to my midsection like icing. Granted, mine has been disappearing the last few weeks. Thanks to my consistency and Dax's help.

"No. You're not a dry, boring muffin. Now, cupcakes?" Dax chuckles low and wipes his hand across his mouth.

Dropping the weight into the weight rack, he stalks to me, a look in his eyes like I'm prey. My heart pumps in my chest like I just did a million of those stupid burpees he makes me do. He doesn't stop at a socially safe distance. No, he gets all up in my post-workout sweaty bubble. I take a step back and knock against the half wall.

"Cupcakes are dangerous."

"Dangerous?" That's not what I expected, and I squint up at him in confusion.

"Yeah. They're my favorite." Somehow the richness in his voice deepens from milk chocolate to sinfully dark.

"Oh?" So, I've written about heroines talking breathlessly and all, but I didn't think it actually happened.

Well, it does.

"They're my kryptonite. Addicting." He leans even closer.

Oh. My. Goodness.

Is Dax Payton going to kiss me?

Me?

Dorky, boring me?

His heat presses in, and drawing air into my lungs is impossible. Just when his lips are a breath from mine, they veer off course, his exhale skimming the skin on my neck. Goosebumps erupt across my body though I'm burning up.

"Just one taste, and I'm a goner." His mouth brushes my earlobe.

I press my palms flat against the wall behind me to keep from grabbing onto him for support. He places his hands on the top of the wall, boxing me in. My knees tremble like I just finished an intense leg day instead of arms. He hesitates, his breath skating along my skin.

Not touching or kissing.

More like torturing.

An appreciative sound rumbles from him. "Very, very addicting."

Finally, his mouth heads towards mine, and I'm either going to pass out or hyperventilate. I just want to lean forward and see if what he says is true. See if he's as hooked on me as he's alluding. Because there's no doubt in what few brain cells remain in my head that I'm in big trouble when it comes to this man.

The bell in the entryway chimes, alerting someone's arrival. Dax pushes off of the wall. His chest heaves as he stares at me with such intense longing I'm about to swoon. He takes two steps back, and the expression slides to a mask of indifference as he glances toward the door.

"Hey, Bill." Dax greets the newcomer with his normal grunt of a hello, gives me one last quick look, then spins on his heel to the free weights still littering the floor.

With shaking muscles, I snatch my bag from the ground, nod at Bill as I pass, and practically run for my car. When I get there, I slide into the driver's seat and grip the wheel with both hands. Staring at my car's reflection in the gym's windows, I try to catch my breath and figure out what the heck just happened.

Chapter Twenty-Four

-Rory-

I relax in my backyard, enjoying the heat of the afternoon sun. Chub's even energized by the day. He snaps at dragonflies as they buzz among the flowers.

I've had plenty of coffee—no sugar, just whipping cream. I've smashed my word count. Somehow, after this morning's workout and almost-kiss encounter (if that's what it actually was), the words flew from my fingertips into the computer. I even caught up on admin for the kennel.

It should be a red banner day. Yet, I feel like that one fish in *Finding Nemo* who's all excited for escape day only to realize the tank's clean, or in my case, my world's still a mess. Part of me wants to just ride the high until the bottom drops out. The other part wants to prep myself for when I'm curled in the fetal position, questioning all my decisions in life.

I've liked being a go-for-it girl the last few weeks. Not worrying so much is freeing. Sure, I haven't been perfect.

Yet, I've tried very hard to cast those cares about my books, my fears, and my need for things to be safe to bigger hands up above, and I don't want to take them back on me.

They're heavy.

"That's it, Chub." I nod at him, and he cocks his head. "I've made my decision. I'm going to be a ride-or-die type woman, not a cower-and-hide one."

He makes a noise like he's blowing a raspberry and goes back to chasing bugs. I'm gonna assume he had something tickling his nose and not that my canine bestie's laughing at me.

I pick my tablet back up and scroll through pixie haircuts on Pinterest. I've been wanting to change my hair for years now, but I just never had the courage. It's hard to change when you've been staring at the same person for almost two decades in the mirror. What if my face looks fat with a short cut? Or glasses and pixie don't mix?

But I'm not worried about what ifs anymore. Besides, it's just hair. If I look like a freak and hate it, I'll just wear a hat until it grows out. It's cold most of the year anyway, so that won't be a problem.

"I think I like the swooped up do, Chub. What do you think?" I turn the tablet to him with the picture of pixie cut a lot like P!nk's, with the top styled high.

Chub turns to me and wags his tail.

"Swooped it is." I smile and slide my finger through a few more. "I've got an appointment tomorrow, so you better be sure."

His entire body wags as he rushes over to me.

I laugh and scoop him up. "I'll take that as a yes."

The doorbell rings, so I set Chub down and head

inside. When I step into the kitchen, the front door opens.

"Rory? You home?" Mark hollers, and my stomach knots like an octopus trying to squeeze into a small opening.

"In the kitchen," I yell back, though part of me wants to hide in the pantry and pretend I'm not here.

After Dax left the party last night, Mark acted weird. He wouldn't talk, hardly stayed near me. But I found him looking at me across the yard several times, and I couldn't read his expression.

I set the tablet on the counter and go to the sink to get a drink. The thought of a confrontation or even awkward conversation makes my throat as dry as the arctic desert. I fill up a glass with water and gulp it down. Instantly, the octopus in my stomach twists and churns.

Note to self: Water and nerves = nausea and possible upchucking.

Mark walks into the kitchen, his gaze instantly connecting with mine and holding. He's calm. Focused. And, to most women, attractive. So, why when I look at him do I only see a friend?

"I'm glad you're here." He casually puts his hands in his pockets and rocks back on his heels. "Did you have a good day?"

"Yeah." I set the glass down, proud my hand doesn't shake, and force a smile. "The sun's shining, so how can it be bad?"

"That's true." He peers out the window for a second before his gaze turns back to me.

I want to shift under the attention, but I stop myself. "You?"

"Oh, you know. Same old, same old. Giving shots and saving lives." He smiles at our old joke.

In truth, Mark's a brilliant vet. When an emergency comes up, he never hesitates with what to do. He's saved so many pets, big and small, he should get an award.

"What's this?" Mark turns the tablet around and scrolls through the pictures I've saved.

"Just some hairstyles I'm thinking about trying."

"What? Why?" He looks up in horror.

"Because I'm ready for a change. I've had this same haircut since middle school." I grab the tablet and shut it down.

"Why change when you look beautiful? You don't work at it, either. You're just who you are. It's why I love you." His words flash bright warning lights off in my head.

"Aah. Thanks, Mark. I love you too." I play it off, hoping he doesn't hear the shake of panic.

"No, Rory. Like 'I love you' love you. Have since that day when we were eight, and we read for hours under the stairs at your parents' cabin." He snorts a self-deprecating laugh and shakes his head. "I just kept waiting for you to realize that I was right here all along, supporting and loving you."

"Mark—"

"From the shocked look on your face, clearly you haven't, and I need to say something now before I lose my chance."

I don't correct him. I have noticed, but saying so would hurt his feelings more.

"Do you think you could love me as more than a friend?" He steps up to me and grabs my upper arms, hope shining from his face.

My breath bottles in my chest. I'm drowning. I can't crush him, not when he's been my friend for so long.

"I don't know." I swallow. "Maybe?"

He cups his hands on my face and kisses me. I gasp in shock, ashamed that I want this kiss to be from someone else. I don't feel anything but sinking dread. I turn my face away and step back.

"Mark, I just—this is all so sudden." I look at him then immediately down at the floor when I see his disappointment.

"That's fine. I'll go." Mark takes a step back. "Take however long you need. I've waited my whole life for you. I don't mind waiting longer."

When the door closes, I stumble back against the counter and crumple to the tiles as sobs tear from my soul. He's my best friend, the one who's always been there for me. I don't think I can tell him the truth, that I won't ever love him as more than a friend, not if it means hurting him.

Chapter Twenty-Five

-Dax-

I cast my line into the water and glance over at Rory for the hundredth time. Ever since I picked her up, she's been completely distracted. Her eyes had been red and swollen like she'd cried for hours. When I'd opened my mouth to ask and she cut me off, I dropped it. But it's been over an hour since we made it to the water, we've caught a dozen fish, and she's still sullen.

Her pole jerks, and she lets out a squeal. Big blue eyes jerk to me in a shocked question. I reel my line in as fast as I can.

"Just crank the reel, Rory. You've got this."

"Holy cow! I don't remember the fish ever being this strong." She yelps as the salmon makes a run for it and the line whizzes fast from the reel.

"Hold on to the handle. Don't let the fish run the line out." I get my hook in and set my rod on the shore.

The two older men standing next to us chuckle, amused at her distress. I shake my head at them and shrug.

"Fishing isn't a good date, young man," one of them offers.

"I don't know, Bert. Seems fishing will show a man the mettle of a woman," the other counters. "My Jean can snag, gill, and gut a salmon better than most men here. And don't get me going on how she handles a halibut."

"Oh, dear Lord. We don't want to know how she handles nothing." Bert shakes his head. "Keep the bedroom doors closed, Earl. There's a lady present."

"Fish, you old git. I was talking about fish." Earl points a finger at Bert. "You're the one with your head in the gutter."

"Thanks, gentlemen," I interrupt before their argument turns into a full out fight. "I appreciate the insight."

"Dax!" Rory calling my name's just about the sweetest sound I've ever heard.

I stifle the urge to wrap her in my arms and kiss her until she's whispering my name so only I can hear. I don't think she'd appreciate that in front of all these people lined up for combat fishing. Her reel spins again. This fish's a fighter.

I step up next to her with the net. "You've got this, Rory."

"No, Dax. I don't." Her body strains against the pull of the salmon. "I'm not strong enough."

"You are." I place my hand on her shoulder for encouragement. "You always have been."

"Seriously. No more mushy talk." She glares at me. "Help!"

I toss the net a few feet from us so we don't trip on it

and step up behind her. The smell of the salty ocean and her sugary sweet scent envelops me as I wrap my arms around her and grab the fishing rod. Her entire body's tense from the strain.

"Okay. We're going to reel as we pull up, then rest as we lower. Ready?" I whisper as she leans into me.

"Yeah."

"Reel, reel, reel," I chant as we lift.

She wasn't kidding. This fish must be massive. I'm not sure I've ever had one on the line this strong while shore fishing before.

"Earl, I take back my comment about fishing not being a good date," Bert says as he walks over and grabs the net. "Looks to me like a smart way to get a woman in your arms."

I laugh as we let the rod down almost parallel to the water. The fish jumps from the water, its scales glittering in the midnight sun. It's a monster. I don't think the line will hold the weight, especially with the fight it's putting up.

"Wahoo, ladies and gents. We've got a king on the line," Bert hollers.

As the fish veers one way then runs the opposite, the people closest to us reel their lines in. The last thing we need is to get tangled up. The pole jerks in our hands, and we both almost lose our grip.

"Brace the end against your hip here." I touch Rory's right pocket. "We gotta keep it tight against your body."

"My arm's giving out." She's breathless, her voice shaking.

I wrap my fingers around her hand and help her

crank the handle. We struggle against the salmon for a millennium before it finally gets close. My muscles burn from the exertion, but I've never had this much fun fishing before.

"Bert, you got that net ready?" I ask, trying not to yell in Rory's ear.

"Just waiting on you two lovebirds to stop cuddling and get that fish in." Bert sounds annoyed, but his smile stretching across his face negates the cross tone.

The rod slips in Rory's hands as she snaps her head to Bert. "Oh, we're not—"

"Focus, cupcake." I squeeze my fingers still covering hers. "We don't want to lose this fish now."

I step back, bringing Rory with me. The salmon's close enough we might be able to drag it to shore. Each step, we reel more line in. Bert's next to us, net at the ready, but I'm not sure if the king will fit.

Bert lunges quick. "Got it."

The net jerks the old man toward the water. I lurch for the net at the same time that Rory does. We collide, and my foot slips on the slick rocks. The ocean rushes toward us. At the last second, I twist so I don't crush Rory against the rocks. Frigid water covers us, shocking my brain and body with intense, icy pain.

She sputters as she pushes up to her knees, grabbing my shirt and dragging me to sit. Her glasses float next to me, so I snatch them before the ocean claims them. She has one hand twisted in my shirt like she's worried I'll go back under and the other's touching my shoulder, my neck, my face, searching for injuries.

"Are you okay? I landed right on you." Her eyebrows furrow over her bright blue eyes.

"I'm fine—"

She gasps, and I tighten my hand on her waist. "The fish!"

"We've got it handled." Earl helps Bert drag the salmon far up the shore.

Her body relaxes with a whoosh. Then she looks at me and giggles. The giggle turns to laughter as she rests her forehead on my shoulder. Fire spreads from my chest to my fingers and toes. I chuckle with her, running my hand up her back and along her neck.

"You're something else, Aurora Wilde," I whisper against her ear, her hair tickling my cheek.

She pulls back, a shy smile on her face as she darts her gaze to the bystanders. She pushes to her feet, tucks her hair behind her ear, and shivers. Then she reaches her hand down to help me up.

"You aren't so bad either, Dax Payton." Her hand's strong in mine and her gaze unwavering as she pulls me up. "Not so bad, at all."

Cheering goes up from those around us. Her shyness returns as she glances at the people watching. I hand her her glasses, and her fingers tremble from the cold. A shiver rushes up my spine as the adrenaline leaches from my body.

"Looks like our fishing trip's done." I step toward the salmon.

"Yeah." Rory's teeth chatter as she puts her glasses on the top of her head.

"This fish of yours is a beaut." Earl toes the fish on the shore.

All his talk of his Jean doing all the work, yet he's already taken care of the fish. He smiles at Rory. She steps up to him and kisses his weathered cheek.

"Thanks for not making me gill it." She pats his shoulder.

"Oh, now. That's no problem at all." Earl's ears redden.

She turns to Bert and does the same. "Thanks for your quick net work."

He clears his throat and puffs out his chest. "Nothing to it."

"Why don't you two hold this beast up so we can take your picture?" Earl points his chin at the salmon.

After handing Earl my phone, I slide my fingers under the gills and heft it up. It has to weigh at least fifty pounds. Rory's eyes go big as she looks from my bicep to the fish and back.

"Come close so we can get the picture and go change." I reach out my free hand, grab her belt loop, and pull her up to me.

"Change? I thought we were done." She trembles against my side.

I smile for the picture. As Earl takes a few more, I turn my face to Rory's hair. Whatever shampoo she uses is stronger with her hair wet.

"Oh, no. We just got started." My lips brush against her ear.

She inhales sharply and looks up at me. "Really?"

There's a hope in her eyes that makes me want to run a victory lap. Her gaze dips to my mouth, and she pulls her bottom lip between her teeth. It takes everything in me not to be a fool and kiss her here in front of all these people.

I flex my fingers on her hip and cock one eyebrow. "You didn't think you'd get out of processing the fish did you?"

Her forehead scrunches. I chuckle and step back so I don't close the short distance between us and kiss her senseless. As her eyes dart from the king hefted next to her and the fish we've already caught, realization sets in, and she slumps with a disappointed huff.

Chapter Twenty-Six

-Rory-

A shiver rushes up my spine as we pull into Dax's drive even though I've already changed. I glance over at Dax in a T-shirt and gym shorts he had in the truck and shiver again. How can he not be freezing?

"The minute we get in, I'll make you some decaf fatty latte." His look's full of concern. "That will warm you right up."

"I'm fine." My teeth chatter.

"Sure." His eyebrow cocks up before he throws the truck in park, gets out, and grabs the cooler of fish from the bed of the truck.

As I follow him to the front door, I take in his yard. It's immaculate, with beautiful green grass. Along the front of the house, pale purple irises and bright yellow poppies beckon me to touch their soft petals.

"So beautiful." I breathe out, reaching to the flower closest to the porch and relishing the velvet between my fingers.

"Yeah." He's staring at me when I look up. "Stunning."

My neck and cheeks warm to the compliment. At least, I think it's a compliment. He clears his throat and motions the cooler to the flowers.

"They're my mom's favorites."

"Well, your mom has great taste." I rush to the door as he jostles the cooler to try to open it.

"Thanks." He steps past me and hauls the cooler to the kitchen.

I'm not sure what I was expecting Dax's house to be like. Probably weights littering the corner, posters of motivational phrases, trophies from past competitions. Definitely a ginormous television on the wall to watch sports on.

What I find's nothing like that. The room's inviting and open, the living room and kitchen blending into one welcoming space. A rich, dark chocolate leather sofa faces two matching armchairs. There's not a tv in sight, only a bookshelf covering the far wall between two large picture windows overlooking the bay and a long table along the wall that I assume leads to the rest of the house.

I meander over to the table and scan the pictures in the frames as the building-pressure sounds of an espresso machine fill the peaceful quiet. There's a couple of Dax as a child with a young woman. She's beautiful, with dark hair like Dax's and the same shape of mouth. She's looking at Dax with such love it makes my insides warm and gooey like cookies fresh from the oven. The rest of the pictures turn me into one big, oozing puddle of mushiness. A few are him and an older woman, probably his grandma, a couple more of his mom, and several of his rugby team. But it's not the team he plays on. No, the pictures are all of the team he coaches.

"You really love coaching, don't you?" I pick one of the pictures up and examine his proud face.

"What I love is giving the kids a chance at something bigger than them, than their circumstances. Rugby changed my life, and I see it changing other's lives as well." He walks into the room with a steaming mug and hands it to me. "For some of these kids, rugby's the only positive thing they have."

"Is that your mom?" I point to one of the woman staring off into the distance, a serene look on her face.

"Yeah. That's her." His voice turns thick with regret, and my heart stutters in my chest.

"Does she live in Seward?" I'm almost too afraid to ask.

"Yeah." His short answer has my breath whooshing out in relief. He places his hand on my elbow, sending another shiver up past my shoulder and into my hair. "Drink your coffee and warm up while I get the cutting boards and knives ready."

"Thanks." I smile, though I'm not cold anymore.

Being in Dax's space has warmed me right up. Still, I don't want to be in his way. He's given me time to peruse his massive bookshelf. Growing up, I always wondered what brought Dax to the library as much as me. I figured he read mystery and horror, storing up new ways to torture me. I never got close enough to actually read the titles.

I scan the bookshelf and gasp in surprise. It's partly filled with business, mindset, and motivational books, which I completely understand. In fact, I have a lot of similar books on my shelves at home. What shocks me is the rest are epic fantasy and romance.

"Romance?" I set my mug on a shelf and look at him.

"Yeah, well, good research." He winks as he plops the cooler on a kitchen chair.

I roll my eyes and scan the titles.

"Truth?" he asks.

"Nah. I prefer lies," I deadpan back at him.

He leans against the counter, vulnerability bunching his shoulders.

"I've always loved reading." He shrugs. "I know. Big shock, the dumb jock reads for fun."

"I never thought you were dumb." I shake my head. "Annoying. Sometimes mean, but never dumb. Not even once."

"Oh. Okay." His shoulders relax.

"You're too quick with witty comebacks to ever be anything less than genius."

His lips tweak up on one side, and his dimple creases his cheek. "Anyway, it's how I escaped life." He shakes his head and stares at his feet. "In high school, I became desperate. All the stories I kept starting were dark and depressing. I lived that every day of my life at home. I needed something that would rescue me from all that, even if for a little while. I found a romance in the free bin at the library and thought 'why the heck not?' I've been hooked ever since."

My eyes dart to the pictures across the room. The few pictures there tell a story of a childhood filled with love. But the memory of that fateful day on the bus in third grade rises, and I remember how beaten down he'd looked. There also aren't any pictures of his dad.

I want to ask more, but Dax has turned his back to

me. I don't want to pry and make him uncomfortable. Skimming the titles, I gasp in delight.

"You have my books?"

All. Of. My. Books.

My eyes rove the shelves greedily. Every single title I've published is here. I never told him my pen name.

"At first I didn't know they were yours, but then you described the bay the same way you had in one of your short stories back in high school, and it all clicked." He walks over, pulls one of my older books from the shelf, and opens to a bookmark. "This one here: The fog skimmed along the ocean like a lover's kiss, barely touching. Teasing. Keeping one guessing whether it would stay or go."

Him reading my words in his deep, sexy voice is almost more than I can handle. I want to toss the book aside, climb up him like a baby monkey, and never let go. Maybe I could get him to narrate all my books. Then I'll get sales just because women want to sit and listen to him. That thought curdles my fatty latte in my stomach.

Scratch that.

I don't want other women listening to him read. No, I want that privilege all to myself.

He closes the book and runs his palm over the cover. "I had already been a fan before, but knowing you wrote them had me buying every book the moment they came out. Reviewed them too. You even used a few of my reviews in your newsletter."

"Really?" I'm smiling like a loon, but I can't help it.

"Yeah. I'm NorthernLightsLover." He twists the book in his hand like he's embarrassed as he sits on the arm of the chair.

"Huh." I scan his bookshelves again, my spines popping out now that I know they're there. "Too bad that horrible reviewer didn't share your thoughts. Maybe then my career wouldn't be on the verge of crashing into the frozen ocean, never to be seen again."

"Didn't you go back and read the comments?"

"Are you kidding me? I read all one hundred and twenty-two replies and watched the viral video on social media. Once was enough to completely eviscerate me and question all my choices." I step back to lean on the bookshelf. "It took me forever to be able to write a decent sentence after that. I was having trouble before, but that review and video destroyed any confidence that I could actually get over my writer's block. That I should even try."

"Then you missed out." He sets the book on the coffee table and wraps his hands around the chair's arm.

"On what?"

"On your fans destroying the reviewer's comments. There may have been people jumping on the bully bandwagon, but there are over 4,000 of your fans sticking up for you. None of the other people she's roasted have had a backlash like she had with you."

"Really?" My chest tightens and eyes sting.

I hadn't been brave enough to look and forbade Jodi from telling me. If I was going to finish my manuscript, I couldn't look at that horrible review again.

"Your readers are wild about you, Rory." Dax shrugs. "Just like I am."

The last tumbles out low, and his eyes soften. I may be clueless when it comes to men, but he's not just talking about books here. Then his reviewer tag hits—NorthernLightsLover. I always searched out his reviews, getting a chuckle out of the coincidence that my real name was Aurora after the aurora borealis, and this reviewer loved northern lights. My lungs labor for each breath like the air's thick and hard to take in. My eyes dart to the book with my words from high school.

"I can't believe you remembered I wrote that all the way back in high school." With it hard to breathe, the words come out a whisper.

"You're a hard one to forget." Dax hangs his head. "No matter how hard I try, I can't seem to get free from you."

"Is that why you teased me in elementary school?" I push my hands into the wood of the bookshelf behind me.

He shakes his head.

"No. You always saw too much, always gave more than you should. I worked so hard at hiding how miserable I was, but you noticed, and I got scared." He glances up at me, an apology in his pained expression. "Your dad was a police officer, and if you told him you thought I wasn't being taken care of, the cops would come and take me away. Then no one would be there to protect my mom. Being mean, picking on you, was a knee-jerk reaction that I regretted the instant your face crumpled, but I couldn't take it back, not when you were so dangerous."

I had never felt dangerous in my life. Cowardly? Absolutely. Bending to others wants even when I desire the opposite? All the time. Keeping things the same so I'll always be safe? Clearly, but doing so only isolated me, pulled me away from who I truly am.

"Dangerous?" My throat tightens, sending pain with each swallow.

His lips pull up on one side, revealing his dimple. "You have this way of drawing me close, pulling me in. When we worked on that project together, I felt comfortable, relaxed."

That didn't sound very romantic. Makes me think of sweatpants or slippers. Comfortable's my entire life wrapped in one word.

"Comfortable?" I lean further against the shelf so my knees don't buckle in disappointment.

"Rory, I never got that as a kid. I always had to be on guard, always, even when I slept. But that time spent with you was like floating carefree in the ocean." He scoffs. "I'm not even sure why I'm telling you this."

He shoves his hand in his hair and leans forward like he's going to stand. I place my palm on his shoulder to stop him. I can't let him change the subject now. He wraps his hands around the chair's arms, his knuckles turning white.

"So, let me get this straight. In elementary school, I was dangerous because I saw too much?" I trace my fingers along the shoulder seam of his T-shirt.

The muscles in his arms bunch, and his voice drops lower. "Yeah."

"In middle school?" I lift one eyebrow in question and step so I'm next to his knees.

"You were scared after the avalanche, and I wanted to protect you." His eyebrows gather in. "So, when I heard people calling you names, I made them stop."

"You did?"

He nods and half shrugs the shoulder under my hand. My fingers tremble along his collar. I had no clue.

"High school?"

"That was the worst." He closes his eyes. "You were

so beautiful and smart, I spent years trying to come up with a way for you to not hate me. But I knew it was wishful thinking."

I step between his knees, tracing my fingers up his neck and along his jaw. His stubble scratches rough on my fingertips, sending sparks up my nerves.

"Now?" I barely whisper.

His Adam's apple bobs against my hand.

"You've ensnared me completely." His gravelly voice sends shivers of delight down my spine. "There's no going back to how my life was before, but I'm afraid going forward with you is just another pipe dream."

I close the last of the distance between us, capturing his lips like he's captured my heart. He follows my lead, but his kiss is hesitant. I want him to wrap me in his strong arms and never let go. His hands stay gripped on the chair. I need words, yet my brain's empty of all but him. I lean my forehead against his and spear my fingers through his hair.

"You make me feel alive, yet safe, Dax Payton, like I've been hibernating in a stinky den and have finally come out from its stifling shadows." I pull back just enough so he can see the truth in my eyes. "I don't want to go back into the dark. I want to stay in the light with you."

His hands spread wide on my back and pull me to him. He buries his face in my neck, each breath sending tendrils of sparks along my skin. The breaths turn to kisses he trails up my neck; each touch lights a fire of nerves. My lungs quit working, and I flex my fingers in his wavy hair.

This sensation's so much more than I ever imagined. I may need to apologize to my characters for not doing it justice. When he finally trails to my mouth, my body's a noodle, only his powerful arms keep me from collapsing to the floor.

"We should stop. Work on fish," he says between kisses.

"Yeah." I turn my head to get a better angle, and my glasses go crooked on my face.

I yank them off and toss them toward the couch. Dax smiles against my lips. My laugh's cut short by his devouring mouth. With a growl, he lifts me from my feet, turns in the chair so he's sitting on the seat, and holds me on his lap.

"The fish can wait," he rumbles in my ear, then scorches my skin until he reaches my lips.

For once, I totally agree.

Chapter Twenty-Seven

-Rory-

The kennel door's bell howls, announcing someone's arrival just as I gather my stuff up to go to the hairdresser. So far, it's been a quiet morning, which is good since I didn't leave Dax's until after two. Cleaning and processing fish takes longer than I remembered, especially when we stopped for kissing.

I smile at the memory of the way he'd cup my neck like I was precious. Sighing, I run my fingers along my skin. It's been very hard getting anything done with how my mind keeps wandering back to him.

"Focus, Rore." Shaking my head, I hike my bag onto my shoulder. "And on what you're supposed to be doing, not Dax's lips."

If I'm going to make it to the hairdresser on time, I need to leave now. I rush out of my office, and practically barrel into Mark. His head hangs on his neck like it's too heavy to hold up. My heart sinks. Had he heard me talking to myself about Dax?

"So, it's true?" Mark's voice cracks.

"What?" Oh, no. He knows.

"That you're hooking up with Dax Payton." Mark's cheek pops as he clenches his teeth.

"We're not hooking up—"

"Don't lie, Rory. There're pictures in the Seward Announcements Facebook group of you and him."

I cringe. Why hadn't I thought about someone posting us catching that king salmon? People give updates on everything in that stupid group. It's great when something important happens, like a missing pet or killer yard sale. Not so great when it comes to gossip.

"We're helping each other. I'm his test subject for a workout program he's creating, and he's taking me on outings for book inspiration."

Why can't I just tell Mark that Dax and I are together?

"Your romance books." He says romance like it's a dirty word, and my shoulders tighten. "Is that why you were at his house until two this morning?"

I gape at Mark. "How do you—"

"Looks like you have a nosy neighbor too." Mark holds up his phone to a video of me pushed up against Dax's truck and him kissing me senseless. "Post reads: Another Wilde daughter living up to her name. Guess the romance author's doing research. Shameful display of PDA."

I gasp, the blood literally freezing in my veins. Why would someone post something like that? I stumble back against the doorjamb and shake my head in shock. I need to contact the admins of the group and see if they can take the post down. I'm starting to really hate social media.

"Why, Rory? Why him of all people?" Mark shoves his phone in his pocket.

"I was wrong about him. There's a lot more to the story than we ever knew." Tears blur my vision as I look at Mark's crushed face.

He shakes his head in disappointment. "You've changed. It's like I don't even know you anymore. You've been lying to me for years. To your *family* for years. Now, suddenly you're talking about chopping your hair off. You won't eat your favorite foods. You're staying until two in the morning at a man's house, a man that you've hated since third grade." He scoffs and rolls his eyes. "Cleaning fish? Yeah. I don't think I believe you anymore."

I jerk at his vehemence. The words cut at my soul, ripping it to shreds that flutter violently in my chest. I can't believe he'd think the worst of me, after all the years we've been friends.

"Don't you ever get tired of doing the same thing over and over again?" I blink to try and clear my tears, but it doesn't help.

"That's called life, Rory."

"No. It's called a rut, and I'm sick of being stuck in it." I push off of the wall. "Changing my hair and the food I eat isn't a bad thing, Mark. And I'm sorry that me being with Dax hurts you. I never, ever would want that. You've been my best friend since second grade."

"Guess that's going to change too, huh?" Mark glares at me and crosses his arms.

I take a deep breath, hating that we're having this conversation. "That's up to you."

"I can't——" His voice cracks, and he jerks his gaze out the window.

His throat bobs once. Twice. I hold my breath, dreading what he'll say. When he does look at me, the anger on his face makes me shudder.

"I've loved you for years, Rory. *Years*. I can't be around you when you're with him." He stomps across the lobby to the door, the howling for the doorbell echoing the sadness crashing over me.

Maybe he's right. My phone dings, and I glance at the haircut reminder on the screen. Am I changing for myself, because I want to, or am I still just hiding behind who I think others want me to be?

Chapter Twenty-Eight

-Dax-

I jog up Rory's drive to her front door, my gaze scanning the direction the video on the Seward Announcement group had to have come from. The curtain moves in the window of the tiny cottage with the bright red door, and my eyes narrow. I never go on social media and wouldn't have even known if Tony hadn't come in gloating that he'd been right about me and Rory.

Within minutes, I'd tracked down the admins and made them remove the post. After the whole reviewer thing, this kind of publicity would upset Rory, especially with the busybody only focusing on the "Wilde daughter" and her "shameful display." The old biddy's the one who should be ashamed.

I take a deep breath and knock on the door. Not so deep inside, I'm worried the attention we've gotten will make Rory pull away. After last night, that's the last thing I want.

The door swings open, and my mouth drops wide.

Rory's hair's cut in a short style like Tinkerbell but swooping up on the top. She's always been beautiful but having her hair away from her face makes her eyes and mouth stand out, like she's been hiding just how stunning she is behind the curtain of blonde.

"You cut your hair." Brilliant, Captain Obvious.

"Yeah."

She fiddles with the back of her head, and my eyes narrow on a word tattooed along her hairline just behind her ear. My gaze zeroes in on it, and Rory suddenly comes into focus. I see her. Not the person she's pretended to be, but the real her.

Her teeth pull on her bottom lip like she's nervous. I want to capture her lip in my own teeth and explore my fingers through her hair. But the neighbor's probably watching, just waiting for another chance to record us.

"It makes your eyes look big," I blurt out.

Her bright blue eyes go wide behind her glasses. She touches her rims and furrows her forehead. I am completely screwing this up.

"Not like frog eyes or anything." I rub my neck that's getting hotter by the second. "They're like how the princesses in the cartoons are now. Sparkling and pretty."

"Oh." Her face crinkles, and mouth twitches in a half smile.

I glance up the street at the red door, then at Rory still standing in her doorway. Her eyebrow cocks in question. Just a sassy lift, and I'm done in.

"Screw it," I mutter as I close the distance between us.

I bend, wrap my arms around the top of her legs,

and pick her up so her face is even with mine. Her laugh as her fingers run along my scalp's the best sound in the world. I step us into her house away from any peeking eyes and push her back against the wall.

Plundering her lips, I barely come up for breath. Not that I need it. I could survive for a long time right where I am. I kiss along her jaw, behind her ear, down her neck. When I finally pull away, her legs are around my waist, the picture that had been hanging on the wall's at my feet, and we're both sucking in air like we just surfaced from free diving.

"You're absolutely gorgeous." I run fingers down her hair and rub my thumb across her tattoo. "Always have been. But something about the way you look now, I finally *see* you, and you're breathtaking." I scoff and drop my head. "You'd think with all the romance books I've read I could come up with something better than that."

"Oh, I don't know." Her voice is airy and full of laughter. "I'd say you're doing a stellar job."

She gives a slight tug on my hair to lift my face and gently kisses me. I cup her cheek in my hand and cherish the moment. It's not as passionate as before, but a part of my soul coils out and tangles within hers, anchoring me to her.

"So, a tattoo?" I tilt her head so I can read it. "Ignite?"

"I got it at my first writer's conference. There's also a fountain pen on the edge of my ear." She turns her head further and moves her ear towards me.

A delicate pen decorates her skin there. I growl and nip her ear. She giggles and tries to pull away.

"You're driving me wild." I kiss the word and straighten.

If we're going to make it to dinner, we need to leave now. I step away from the wall and reluctantly put her down. But I'm not ready to let her go completely. I trail my hand down her arm and thread my fingers through hers.

"What does ignite mean?" I lead her outside, locking and closing the door behind us.

Chub snuck out to the front porch while we made out in the entryway. He's staring at us like he's not amused. I scoop him up and tuck him under my free arm. He might as well come with us. Rory smiles up at me, inflating my ego even more, then scratches Chub's head.

"Well, there was this author named Wilfred Peterson who was an inspiration to me as a writer." She shrugs. "I already felt like a rebel writing in secret, and I had this idea for a tattoo, so I thought, 'Why not?' Back there, no one will see it."

She cringes up at me.

"That's not the case now." I chuckle.

"No, but all of my secrets are out. I might as well embrace who I've felt I am on the outside, not just the in."

"I love it." I clamp my mouth shut before I confess more.

"I got a new tattoo every conference I went to."

I twist our joined hands behind her and pull her close. "You have more?"

"Not many, and they're hidden."

The thought of being the first—no, the only person to see her other tattoos makes me want to throw all logic and convention out the window and whisk her to the courthouse.

"You're killing me, Wilde."

I peck her on the cheek and push her toward the truck. After she's situated with Chub in her lap, I shut the door and run around the hood. We're definitely late for dinner.

"You never told me what ignite means." I reverse out of the driveway and head across town.

"'Walk with the dreamers, the believers, the courageous, the cheerful, the planners, the doers, the successful people with their heads in the clouds and their feet on the ground. Let their spirit ignite a fire within you to leave this world better than when you found it.'" Goosebumps erupt along my skin as Rory inhales like she's breathing in the words she just spoke and exhales slowly. "Wilfred Peterson's words fueled me to pursue my dream of writing. I used to repeat those words to myself every morning when I got up, pumping me up, reminding myself to have courage and dream. Ignite was my first tattoo because I want my words to leave this world better, even if all they do is bring readers joy for however long it takes them to read my book."

"See." I reach across the console and wrap my hand around hers. "Breathtaking."

She tucks her head and smiles. With both of her hands, she clutches mine. Chub sighs and rests his chin on top of them.

"So, where are we going?" She glances out the window.

"How does dinner with my mom sound?"

Her hands flinch around mine. I hold my breath. It's a big step in a relationship that's so new. I probably should have asked earlier, but I didn't want her to say no. I'd hoped she'd be excited, but her legs suddenly bouncing Chub enough to give him Shaken Doggie Syndrome probably means she's not as ready for this as I am.

Chapter Twenty-Nine

-Rory-

We pull up to a beautiful two-story house with a plaque next to the front door that reads Eagles Nest Assisted Living. Two men, probably in their eighties, sit on the front porch, staring at a checkers board on the table between them. While the house, yard, and flowers are just as neat and tidy as Dax's, the sign on the siding has my stomach tying knots upon the knots already there.

Am I meeting his grandma too?

Meeting Dax's mom has all kinds of nerves kicking up, but the possibility of meeting both his mom and grandma at the same time might just make me throw up. Hopefully not in the azaleas. What if they don't like me? What if the women smiling at Dax in those pictures take one look at me and instantly peg me as not worthy? I stare at the bright, robin's egg blue door and try to gather the courage I felt when I left my house.

"Before we go in, I need to warn you about my mom." He's not helping one bit.

I turn to him, trying to relax my death grip on Chub. Be brave, Rore.

"Okay." My voice cracks, and I inwardly cringe.

He taps his thumb on the steering wheel, huffs out a breath, then starts talking without looking at me. "The summer after we graduated, I came home late one night to my mom in a pool of blood and my dad gone."

Shock crashes over me, rushing my nerves away to leave only pain for Dax and the beautiful woman in the picture.

"No." I cover my mouth with one hand and touch Dax's arm with the other.

He covers my hand, then takes it in his. He's examining it while he talks, like running his fingers and eyes along the length of each line helps him get the story out.

"For years, we'd lived with his abuse. If one of us was hurting, the other would draw his attention to keep injuries to a livable level. Mine were always easy to hide once I started playing rugby."

My heart aches for that young Dax I grew up with. Even in third grade he was the protector, picking on me so I wouldn't notice his bruises and tell my dad. No child should ever live with that pain and fear. No *person* should. He draws a swirl in my hand, then threads his fingers through mine and squeezes tight.

"That night, I finally had enough. I wasn't taller than him, but I was stronger. When he got drunk and started hitting Mom, I lost it. Beat him up and knocked him out. Mom told me to leave. To cool off. I was only gone an hour, maybe two before I came back. Mom almost died. Would have if I hadn't come back when I did."

He pauses, swallowing, and I have to ask. "Did your dad go to jail?"

His head shakes, bottoming out my gut. "They never found him."

"What?"

That doesn't make sense.

It's not like there are a lot of ways to leave Alaska.

"We don't know if he wandered off into the woods and died or if he's hiding like the coward he is. I hope it's the first, but I'm not that lucky." Dax's cheek flexes. "I should've stayed. Called the cops. Shouldn't have let him hurt my mom for so many years."

"No, Dax. You can't put that on yourself." I scoot up against the console, making Chub groan on my lap and press his hand between both of mine. "You were just a child."

"Not by then, Rory." He spears me with a tortured gaze. "I could have stopped him years before, but I didn't. Now Mom has permanent brain damage and has to live in assisted living. She's not even sixty, Rory."

"So, that's why you didn't go play rugby professionally?" My heart breaks into a million pieces for him.

"I couldn't leave after that." He shrugs. "She needed me, and I couldn't let her down again."

Earlier he said he finally saw me. I can't explain the emotions rushing through me better. It's like someone has turned the flood lights on Dax Payton, and he's blinding. My body pops and sizzles like a hundred sparklers have been set off inside me. I lean over the console and kiss him, pouring all my pain, respect, and attraction for him into the tender touch. I pull away just enough to speak.

"I think I'm in trouble." My lips brush his.

He squeezes my hand. "Why's that?"

"Because I'm falling in love with you, Dax Payton," I whisper the words as fear snakes its cold fingers into the sparkling warmth flooding me.

He shifts his head and cups my cheek but doesn't get any closer. "And that's trouble?"

"It's a plot twist, something I never planned."

A sharp rapping on the window jerks me back to my seat. Those sparklers transform to hot embarrassment that rushes up my neck and singes my cheeks. One of the old men from the porch scowls at us through my window.

"Knock it off. I'd like to eat while I'm still young and have my own teeth." He shakes his head and turns to the house. "I warned that boy about distracting women."

Dax laughs as he opens his door. "Guess we should head in."

I gather up Chub from where he's still sleeping on my lap. He snorts, then goes back to snoring. By the time Dax comes around the hood and opens the door, I've got my heart rate under control. One half-smirk from him as he helps me out picks it right back up.

"Don't mind Virgil. He's just cranky he never found a woman worth getting distracted over." Dax wraps his fingers through mine, and those sparklers light right back up in my chest.

Virgil shakes his head as he hobbles up the path. "Fool boy. Ruin everything."

"Hey, Coach." The young girl from rugby practice waves at us from the next door house's porch.

Just great.

I clench my teeth together and inwardly groan. Did

the entire world witness me practically climbing over the console to make out with Dax? He jiggles my hand in his and chuckles.

"Hey, Skye. I didn't realize you live here." He pulls me to the low picket fence separating the two houses.

"We just moved in." She sniffs and glances over her shoulder to her front door.

Someone inside's crying. Tires squeal down the road, and Skye's gaze jerks that way. The hairs on the back of my neck rise, sending a shiver down my back.

"Everything okay, Skye?" Dax noticed it too.

Skye glances back to the house, then jogs over to the fence. How this petite thing plays rugby with boys twice her size is beyond me. I wish I had her courage.

She grabs a fence plank and kicks the bottom of it. "My Aunt Marie's ex-husband went to her house. They got divorced earlier this year. She was done being his punching bag, but I guess he didn't get the memo. She's hurt pretty bad."

I gasp. "Chip and Marie?"

Skye spears me with a suspicious look. "Yeah."

Marie's been my sister Denali's friend since high school. We all knew Chip was a jerk, but I didn't think he actually hit her.

"Is Marie okay?" I look toward the house.

"Yeah. She will be once the cops find Chip." Skye looks down the street again. "He'll go to jail for this, so that should make things easier on Marie."

If they find him.

"I can stick around here until he's caught." Dax tips his head to his mom's place. "Nancy, the owner of this place, has a comfy couch she'll let me crash on."

I peek up at him. This must be bringing back so

many memories for him. I step closer, wanting to show him he's not alone anymore but also needing his warmth and strength.

"Nah. Some ex-hockey player named Nathan's hanging around." Skye must not know just what a big deal Nathan Blaine is.

How did my sister's ex-boyfriend get dragged into this mess?

"Why's Nathan here?" I have to ask, and, seeing that Skye's full of info she's willing to spill, I might as well take advantage.

"He was taking his kid to Marie's for falcon training when he found her." Skye shrugs. "I think he'll do, Coach. I mean, even if he's just a hockey player."

"Better than a football player." Dax wraps his arm around my waist.

"Ain't that the truth." Skye smiles and rolls her eyes.

"Call me if you need anything, and I'll be here." Dax steps toward the house. "We better get in before Virgil has a fit."

"Thanks, Coach. Good luck on the tournament tomorrow."

"Thanks," he answers.

I look one last time toward Skye's house, my heart aching for Marie. She's the sweetest person, always so giving, even in high school. How long had Chip been abusing her? I shake my head and lean into Dax. At least she hadn't stayed as long as Dax's mom had.

"You okay?" I ask as we step up the porch.

"Yeah." He glances over as Skye rushes through her front door. "Just wondering if I should stay here anyway."

"Nathan won't let anything happen to them, even if

he's just a hockey player." I place my hand over Dax's heart. "But if you're going to stay up all night worrying about it, then you should."

He opens the screen as he sighs. "No, Skye's dad will be there at night, and he's ex-military. Marie should be safe, hockey player and all."

I laugh as I walk past. "Where's your tournament this weekend?"

"Up in Anchorage. I'd love for you to come. I can get you a room." He grasps my hand back in his, and my heart soars.

"I'd like that."

He smiles at me, a full on, two-dimpled smile that makes me want to push up onto my toes and kiss right where his cheeks crease. Since we've already been caught locking lips by more people than I care to think about, I push the urge down and finally scan the house. Good thing I refrained, because there are five people sitting around the dining table staring at us. My cheeks heat at the scrutiny.

Dang it.

I was hoping I'd have a modicum of grace and dignity when I met his mom. No. Her first impression of me is me ogling her son's dimples.

"Told you he's hopeless," Virgil mutters loud enough for me to hear across the room. "You joining us or just going to stand there gawking at each other?"

"Virgil!" A woman in her fifties snaps Virgil with her napkin. "Mind your manners when you're at my table."

Dax leads me across the room. I force myself to loosen my death grip on his hand and take a deep breath. There's nothing for me to be nervous about. If I remind myself of that a few more times, maybe I'll actually believe it. Dax introduces everyone, saving his mom for last.

"Everyone, this is my girlfriend, Rory Wilde."

I jerk in surprise at his claim. We hadn't actually discussed what the status of our relationship is, but hearing him call me his has my heart soaring higher than the eagles in the cove. His hand flexes on my hip, and he tenderly kisses the side of my head.

"You okay?" he whispers.

"Absolutely." I smile up at him.

His mom stands and gives me a hug, then tells me to sit next to her. I'm so full of joy I could do a hundred burpees and not be winded. As the food's passed, his mom leans forward so she can see Dax around me.

"I like her, Dax. Her energy's beautiful." She's not quiet with her declaration.

I'm not sure if that's because of her brain injury or if she's always been so forthright. Either way, my ears burn, and I'm half wishing I'd waited to chop off my hair. Dax's hand goes to my knee and squeezes.

"It always has been." Dax winks at me.

All my nerves evaporate with those four little words.

Chapter Thirty

-Dax-

Pain spikes through my side as the opposing team's ten slams into me. I hit the ground, smacking my head on the grass. Stars explode in front of my eyes, but I shake them off and scramble to get up.

"Get your head on, Dax," Tony yells as he rushes past.

The match only has two minutes left. We're winning, but not by much. One try from the opposing team will change that.

I sprint down the pitch. If we lose this match, then the weekend's over. While losing sucks, it's part of the game. It may be high-schoolish of me, but I don't want to get the smack down the first match Rory watches.

Tony smashes into the forward carrying the ball, and I rush into the breakdown. If we can form the ruck fast enough, we'll take possession of the ball. I'd feel a whole heck of a lot better if the ball was on the other end of the pitch far away from our opponent's try line.

I step over Tony as he rolls out of the ruck, drop

lower than the dude protecting the ball, and slam into the man, binding to his hips. He staggers back but recovers. I'm pushing with everything in me to get the advantage. The ball bounces against my ankles, and I drive harder, stepping over the ball so it's behind my legs.

Pete darts in, snatches the ball up, and tosses it back to Cook who takes off toward our try line. The ruck breaks, and I stumble from the release of pressure.

The whistle blows.

Game over.

We won … barely.

My gaze zeroes in on the bleachers as I lean over my knees to catch my breath. Rory jumps up and down, her fingers between her lips as she whistles. I've never seen her so excited or wild, and victory fills my chest with energy. I'd love to race up the bleachers and celebrate by kissing her until everything else disappears. I straighten and take a step toward her when a shoulder slams into mine.

"Forgetting something?" Tony glares at me and heads to shake hands with the opposing team.

Right.

I wave at Rory and head to the other team. There will be plenty of time for celebrating later. After shaking hands, we make our way to the locker room. I'm not two steps in the hallway, and Tony's up in my face.

"What's with you, man?" He's always been a hothead but never with me.

"Back off, Tony." I step around him.

He grabs my jersey. "You almost lost us the game because your head kept swiveling to the stands."

"I was off, okay. Tomorrow'll be better." I jerk my shoulder from his grip.

"So, what, you get a little attention from the pussy cat and everything else comes in second?" Tony's question burns in my chest.

"Don't call her that." I grit my teeth, determined not to punch my best friend in the face.

"I didn't realize you were so desperate for affection that a little action from Rory would turn you obsessed." Tony spreads his arms wide. "Hit it and move on, man. We have too much on the line for you to be distracted right now."

"It's not like that with her."

"Seriously?" Tony's look of disbelief would be comical if I wasn't so angry.

"Drop it, okay. Just back off, Tony. I was off today. Sue me." I turn away from him. "I'll be on tomorrow."

And I will be. There's no way I'll let my team down again.

"You don't get it, do you?" Tony pushes me into the wall, and I can hardly hear what he says next over the rage roaring in my ears. "Ever since you started working out with her, you're losing focus. Keep it up, and the gym will be what takes the next hit. You have plans, Dax. Goals we all have worked our butts off for. Don't lose all of that over a jump in the sack."

I burst from his hold and slam him up against the opposite wall. "Don't talk about her like that. Don't even joke."

Tony may have no qualms with sleeping around, but he knows I won't cross that line.

"Don't ruin everything over a girl," he shouts back.

"Hey! Hey!" Pete jams in between us. "Knock it off you two."

I push Tony as I move away. Stomping down the hall, I slam into the locker room. He's wrong.

Dead wrong.

Rory's not distracting me from what's important. I jerk my jersey off as an inkling that Tony might be right slips in. I shake it off. I know what my priorities are.

Chapter Thirty-One

-Rory-

You know when something was never really on your radar as a thing you'd enjoy and you dismiss it without really much thought? Like meatballs with jalapeño cranberry sauce or watching curling on TV. You don't think you'd become addicted with just one exposure, but you do.

Yeah, that's rugby.

It's the most intense sport I've ever witnessed. I got a workout just from how tense I was while watching. Not only that, but the uniforms can't be beat. Dax's shorts hug his legs and backside so tight, I now have an even better understanding of just how powerfully built he is.

I peek over at him as he finds a parking spot in the hotel lot. He's been quieter than I thought he would be after a win. He catches me staring and smiles. Funny how a month and a half ago I would have been mortified. Now, I tip my mouth up on one side and give what I hope's a come-hither look.

"I'm glad I came. I think I may just have to write a

rugby series. You were quite the inspiration." I wag my eyebrows.

His smile falters, but he puts the truck in park, leans over, and presses a kiss in that spot I've come to realize he likes below my ear. "I'm glad you came too."

My face hurts with joy and my body hums. Make out session in the car, here we come! No chance of the neighborly snoop seeing us here. His phone dings with a voicemail, and he pulls away. My body slumps against the seat as the hum turns to discordant gongs with each heartbeat.

"Huh. Wonder why it didn't ring?" he mumbles as he taps the voicemail icon.

Since the truck's still running, the replay comes through the truck speakers.

"Dax, I understand not sending results from your guinea pig, though I'm not happy about being put off." Something in the man's voice makes me dislike him instantly.

I lift an eyebrow at Dax.

"Vince, the president of the investment group I'm working with." Dax shrugs, but there's a tightness in his shoulders that wasn't there before.

"What I don't understand is how I still don't see squat on your social media feed. The few videos you've posted aren't going to cut it. You need to be out there, not your gym. *You.* I want——"

Dax taps off the voicemail and deletes it with a huff. The way the man talked had all kinds of self-preservation instincts firing. If I was Dax, I wouldn't want to work with a jerk like that.

"He sounds lovely." I can't keep the comment in.

"Yeah, well, if I want this expansion to happen, he's

a necessary evil." Dax turns the truck off, grabs his wallet, and jerks the door open.

All sparkles and joy from a moment earlier fizzled and died with that interruption. Dax smiles at me through the windshield, and I shake off the feeling of disappointment. He has to be exhausted after that brutal match. I know I am. Then to get that voicemail from a man who is less than pleasant? I shake my head at my selfishness. I don't understand all Dax has going on, but I know it's important to him. There'll be plenty of time for make-out sessions throughout the weekend.

I roll my eyes. I sound like a hormone-filled teen. Guess that's what happens when you sequester yourself away from the opposite sex and forget to date. No wonder my muse took off for a more hopping locale. She had to have been bored out of her mind.

He opens my door and gives me a hand out. As we walk to the tailgate, he rolls his shoulder. With all the hits he took, he must be sore.

"I could give you a massage."

Bold, Rore.

Maybe too bold.

Do I honestly think rubbing my hands along his muscles is a good idea? He freezes as he opens the camper shell hatch. He clears his throat and lowers the tailgate.

"As much as I like the thought of a massage from you …" He lifts my hand and kisses my fingers. "I made a promise to myself in high school that I wouldn't go beyond kissing until I was married."

"You did?" I gape at him, too astonished to cover my reaction.

"Shocking, I know." He shrugs. "My mom married

my dad because she got pregnant with me right before graduating high school. I don't want to be stuck with someone for life over a one-night stand or even something more when I'm not completely committed. The easiest way for that not to happen is by not tempting myself with more than I can handle. You, Cupcake, I can barely handle stopping at kissing. Massage, in a hotel room? Restraint destroying."

The hum's back, only this time, it's vibrating my entire body with happiness.

"Don't look at me like that." He reaches into the truck bed and pulls out his duffle. "That's almost as difficult to overcome as a massage."

I turn to get my suitcase, stifling my smile as best as I can. There's no use, though. Jubilation electrifies all my cells.

Thanks to Alaska's swooping roads, my suitcase has jostled to the far end of the bed. Dax reaches for it but flinches with a groan.

"I've got it." I hop into the back of the truck—which I can do with ease now—and push the suitcase toward him.

When he grabs my waist to help me down, I spear my fingers through his hair, still wet from his shower, and kiss him. Up here on the tailgate, we're almost eye level. The touch exhilarates my cells even more, making them full of love and happiness. They drink it in like they've been parched, and their vitality rushes through me.

He roughly crushes me to him. I tug on his hair, and he growls. Growls! A shiver runs down my back. Never thought a sound like that would actually cause a reaction, but, oh man, I love it.

Kisses trail along my jaw toward my ear. He buries his face against my neck, his harsh breath warming my skin. His chest heaves against mine, like he's just rushed across the pitch for an hour.

"Trouble." He kisses my neck, pulls back, and cups my cheek in his palm. "Big trouble."

He rubs his thumb along my lower lip once. Twice. Three times. I'm on edge, desperate for him to dive right back in but, also, a very small part of me hoping he won't. His resolve's stronger than mine, and, in this moment, I need his strength.

"Come on." He wraps his arm around my waist and lifts me off the tailgate. "Let's go get checked in, then we'll grab dinner … somewhere very public."

I snort a laugh as he threads his hand through mine and pulls me to the hotel. When we get inside, I stumble over my feet as two kids race right in front of us. The lobby's in chaos. Stacks of duffle bags and kids in jerseys dot the area. Adults with binoculars and maps fill the couches and chairs.

"This can't be good." Dax snakes us through the mess of people to the front desk.

He huffs and shifts on his feet as we wait. His thumb taps a nervous beat against the back of my hand. When the man behind the desk waves us up, Dax hurries forward.

"Dax Payton checking in, and I need to get a second room, please."

"Funny one." The man laughs, and Dax's Adam's apple bobs. "We don't have any rooms available."

"Seriously?" Dax slumps against the desk and hands over his driver's license and credit card.

"Man, look around. On top of the normal summer

tourist craziness, there's a statewide soccer tournament, a birding convention, and a rugby championship. There aren't any rooms in all of Anchorage." The attendant taps rapidly on his keyboard and shifts through the box of keycards waiting in envelopes. "You're just lucky you booked your room months ago."

"Sorry." Dax darts a glance at me, then bends low. "I can sleep in the truck."

"Don't be silly." I love how serious he's about this. "We're both adults. I think it'll be okay."

I pat his arm, but he closes his eyes and shakes his head. Chuckling, I rise up on my tiptoes. He wraps his arm around me when I teeter.

"I promise I won't do anything tempting," I whisper, then fall back on my heels.

"Not possible, Rory." He laughs and takes the keycards.

We find the elevators, only getting run into once. The poor kid will probably be terrified for life with how Dax spears him with a glare. As we cram into the elevator, I have to press against Dax's side for everyone to fit.

"You won't believe what the hotel did." One of the soccer moms complains to another. "They put us in a room with one bed. We were planning on cramming three kids in one of the beds, but now I don't know what I'm going to do."

One bed?

Dax hadn't expected to have a roommate when he reserved his room. With his size, he had to have gotten a king bed.

Is it possible I might be in my very own one bed trope?

I duck my head to hide my excitement as the moms

get off the elevator. I've written this trope a dozen times, at least. It's one of my favorites. The intimacy and struggle of sharing a bed's undeniable.

We arrive at our floor, and my heart picks up to a gallop. My pulse chants *one bed, one bed, one bed* loudly in my ears. Dax wipes his hand across his forehead. Why's he sweating? The air conditioner's on. The green light flashes on the lock, and I hold my breath.

Two beds.

Air whooshes out in immense disappointment.

"Oh, thank you, Jesus for hotel mistakes." Dax's voice has far too much relief in it.

"Excuse me?"

"I know all you romance writers love throwing your characters into one bed." He tosses his bag on the closest bed and flops down next to it, laying his arm over his face like the relief took everything out of him. "You're distracting enough across the room. Sharing a bed would kill me."

I tweak my lips and glide into the room. Okay. So we don't get the trope. If he keeps saying things like that, I won't miss the one-bed at all.

Chapter Thirty-Two

-Dax-

Shoulder bones grind into mine as the scrum shifts back and forth over the ball. This team's full of brutes quick on their feet, with half their line as big as me. Last year, we barely won the championship over them.

Today?

It's a real battle.

Doesn't help that I spent half the night watching Rory in the soft light the clock made. The scrum shifts, and Tony grunts next to me.

"Come on, Dax. Push." He's been on me like a cranky old man, snapping barbs all game like I can't keep focused on my own.

Gritting my teeth, I dig in harder, putting all my strength into shifting the scrum in our favor.

"Got it." Cook huffs, as he maneuvers the ball between his legs.

Our number eight's on it. A collective heave of relief ripples through the jumbled mass of men a second before everyone snaps into action. I rush toward the ball our team moves down the pitch. My eyes track the ball as it gets tossed backward from one teammate to another. Any second, I might need to catch it or guard it, and both need my concentration to calculate the outcome and quickly adjust.

Movement in the bleacher next to the turquoise shirt that's been in my peripheral all match draws my gaze away. A yell and the ball skipping across the pitch snaps it right back. Pete scoops up the ball and takes off at a diagonal for the sideline, which puts my eyes right on Rory.

There's a guy from one of the other teams sitting next to her. Her arms are crossed, and she's shaking her head at something he's saying. All match she's been the picture of joy, cheering and carrying on. This switch in her has me burning in rage.

The ball smacks into my chest a moment before a body slams into it. I crash to the ground. A crack, like a thick branch snapping in the woods, sounds as another player lands on me. Pain rushes up my arm, making my vision dance with popping stars.

No.

Not now.

The other players tumble off me and take off down the field, but I can't move. I lay there with my face against the turf. Grass tickles my nose, but all I care about is the agony my arm's in. Easing onto my back, I try to move my fingers, but stop when jabs of pain knife in my forearm.

"I warned you, man." Tony stomps up. "She's ruined everything."

I growl, glaring up at him as the medic runs up. "Back off."

They fuss over me, telling me what I already know. I've broken my arm and need to go to the hospital. Game over.

Rugby season finished.

All because I let my attention slip.

I walk off the field toward the ambulance. Rory waits there. Her eyes are wide with worry behind her glasses. The closer I get I can see her better through my blurred vision. Her cheeks glisten with tears that she quickly wipes away when I step up to her.

"Dax?"

There's so much in that one word—pain, concern, love. The only other person I've felt that from was Mom. Since that night so many years ago, even she hasn't had much concern for me.

"I'm okay." I reach out my good hand and pull her next to me. "It's just a broken arm."

"Just a broken arm?" Her laugh lacks humor, and she wraps her arms around me like I need help walking.

"It'll be fine." I kiss the top of her head. "Just will have to ride the humiliation train when videos of the hit spread across social media."

"Why would it do that?" She looks at me in horror.

I laugh but cut it short when even that hurts. "That's part of the sports and fitness community. If you do a bonehead move that ends you in the hospital, it's like free publicity."

"That's horrible."

"That's life," I mumble, the pain making even talking hurt.

"Want me to drive you to the hospital?" She looks up at me. "Or I can follow the ambulance and meet you there."

She glances toward the sidelines. Her forehead scrunches as she thinks things through.

"I can get one of your water boys to show me your locker and get your keys."

"Ride with me in the ambulance." I lean on her like I need her help. "We'll get a cab later."

Her grip on my jersey holds tight the entire walk to the ambulance. She steps back to let the paramedics load me in. One wave from me, and she scrambles through the door and sits on the small bench next to my head.

The paramedics do their thing as the vehicle takes off. I don't really notice any of it. How could I when Rory leans over me, her fingers running through my sweaty hair? She starts blabbering on about her latest book and how she's almost done. She talks about her nephew and the time he broke his leg climbing a tree to save a baby bird from the neighbor's cat.

And all the time she's chattering on, her fingers don't stop caressing. She dips down and kisses my forehead. My lips. Her touch is better than any painkiller, including the morphine dripping into the IV.

Is she a distraction?

Absolutely. My busted arm proves that. She trails her fingers along my jaw, and I close my eyes to the soothing sensation.

But what if she's a distraction I want?

Chapter Thirty-Three

-Rory-

I didn't think Dax would want to work out this morning, but I should've known a broken arm wouldn't stop him. Glancing over at his shirtless self holding the warrior pose, I smile at the black cast covering his right forearm. In his drugged-up ramblings, he'd said black was manly, but then only half-heartedly protested when I bought the white Sharpie and drew flowery tattoos over it. He'd even added his own.

D hearts A.

I bite my lip. Dax loves Aurora? He hasn't come out and said it, but every touch and heated glance makes me think it's true. I wobble in my pose.

"Focus, Wilde." He forces exasperation.

"Sorry." I weakly pretend contriteness.

I just can't right now. Too much energy rushes through me to stand still. I just did an insane workout I never thought I'd be able to do. The gorgeous man next to me might love me. He, at least, really likes me. My book's practically writing itself, and even the drama on social media has fizzled to a stop.

Life couldn't get more perfect.

"You know what? I'm not sorry. Not one bit." I dance around him, shadow boxing as he shakes his head. "I feel incredible. I finally feel like I could take on the world instead of just hide from it. Finally feel like I might not be such an outcast."

"Outcast?" That gets him out of his pose. "You weren't ever an outcast."

"Have you seen my family?" I laugh and shake my head. "I love them, but do you know how hard it is to come from a family of larger-than-life heroes and be so completely dull you disappear?"

The words hover above me, siphoning my joy into its dark cloud. "You have no idea what it's like being a coward. That avalanche made my cousins and sister want to be in the wild, helping others. All I wanted to do was hide behind my books," I say.

"I've always seen you, Rory. Always." His good arm wraps around my waist, and he kisses my neck.

I cup my hands around the back of his head and press my lips against his. Sweat fills my senses. I've grown to love that smell. It's the scent of victory. Of overcoming. I smile against his lips and give him another peck before pushing him away.

"Stop distracting me. I've got pull ups to conquer." I swing my arms and tip my head from side to side as I line up to my nemesis—the pull-up bar. "I'm smashing out ten today."

"Ten?"

"Yeah. Yeah. I know I've been stuck at six, but I'm

feeling like I can do it today." I stare the bar down. "Your mine today, buddy."

"Did you just trash talk the bar?"

"Yeah, and now it's shaking in fear."

Dax laughs low behind me. The sound swirls in my belly, tempting me to forget about the pull ups and see how many reps of a lip workout we could get in before someone arrives. I huff out the swerve in my resolve and reach for the metal above my head. Besides, a celebratory make out session will be more satisfying.

Dax's arm wraps around my waist, making my resolve swerve even more, and lifts me up to the bar. "Up you go, Rocky."

I push all thought from my brain and use his lift to start my momentum. The first two reps glide up and down smoothly. The third has heat spreading between my shoulder blades. The fifth turns the heat to sharp, stabbing pain.

"You've got this, Cupcake." Dax's voice pitches low, like he's worried he'll break my concentration.

With the sixth pull up, my arms tremble. That usually starts two pull ups before I'm out. I growl through the seventh. The bar's going to get the knockout; I can feel it.

"Come. On." I'm halfway up the eighth, but my muscles won't budge any further.

Just when I'm going to drop and admit defeat, Dax's right hand grabs the bar next to mine. His legs wrap loosely around my waist and his body's hot against my back. Then, he lifts a one-armed pull up and gives me just enough boast to finish the rep. We look silly in the mirror, like an ape getting a piggyback ride from an orangutan, but I couldn't care less. I want this man's strength.

"Eight." His whisper brushes my neck.

I close my eyes to the sensation of being supported by him. When I get to the bottom of the exercise, I pull up again. My arms scream for me to stop, but he lifts with me, giving me just enough help to push past my weakness.

"Nine," I ground out. "One more."

I groan as my muscles along my upper back feel like they're about to rip apart. My entire body trembles as I pull higher. Just when my muscles scream for mercy, Dax's presence lifts me past the point my muscles stall. The sharp tang of metal fills my nose as my chin clears the bar.

"Ten." I puff out, and slowly lower myself like he taught me.

His legs unwrap around mine, and cool air blows across my skin. I hang for a moment, relishing the victory and sensation of Dax's help. He walks around in front of me, tapping my hip with his casted hand as he passes.

"You did good, Wilde."

He's smiling, pride beaming from him. This is definitely a time to celebrate with copious kissing. Adrenaline rushing, I swing my legs up and wrap them around his waist, then I reach up and hold onto the top of his shoulder. His arms wrap around my back, and I let go of the bar.

"Thanks." I don't get the entire word out before I'm kissing him.

My body relaxes against his. The reward of a killer

workout hums along my muscles, making them that satisfied ache. He holds me up easily, even with his broken arm, and walks backward as we celebrate in spectacular fashion. When his back hits the mirror, he leans against it for support.

His hand skims along the skin on my back where my shirt's pulled up slightly. I shiver and tug on his lower lip with my teeth. He growls, turning that shiver into dancing northern lights across my body.

How could I have ever thought this man vile?

He's warmth and strength.

Heart and dedication.

He could use his power to harm, to muscle his way to get what he wants, but he only helps others. I spear my fingers through his hair as he trails his lips along my jaw. I don't want to ever let go. I want to spend the rest of my life wrapped in his love.

Maybe I can follow Violet's lead and run off to Vegas.

The front door clicks. Dax groans and buries his face into my neck. A blush heats my cheeks, but I'm not mortified like I used to be. I unwrap myself and smile up at him as he lets me down.

"Not bad for a one-armed man." I wink.

"Guess all those kissing scenes you wrote came in handy," he shoots back and wags his eyebrows.

"Speaking of, I should get going. My book's due to the editor in less than a week." I can't resist and step in for one last, quick kiss. "See you tonight?"

"Absolutely."

Joy floods me at his immediate answer. I turn to get my stuff and spy Dax's friend, Tony, at the front desk.

He's thunking stuff onto the counter. He's never been a favorite of mine. In fact, in school, he could be downright mean. I never realized how most everyone's teasing stopped in middle school, except Tony's. His was more underhanded, jabs under his breath instead of out for everyone to hear. Maybe as Dax's best friend, Tony had needed to push Dax's enemy more than the others had? Whatever the case, that was years ago. If I want to be in Dax's life, I have to make nice with his friends.

I grab my stuff and head to the door. "Morning, Tony."

"Morning," he mumbles, not looking at me.

"Listen, Tony, I know we weren't friends in school, but I'm hoping we can be friends now." I smile and lift a shoulder in question.

"Sure thing, Rory." Tony returns the smile, his gaze darting to Dax then back to me. "At first, I thought you'd ruin him, distract him from what we've killed ourselves over. Now, though, I think you're exactly what he needed to get the gym to the next level."

I turn my gaze to Dax. He's still leaning against the mirror watching us. He lifts an eyebrow, his expression asking if I'm okay. I give him a small smile in return and look at Tony.

"Good. He's helped me too."

He chuckles, his lip lifting on one side like there's something more to my comment than face value. I push my unease away. If I'm going to get along with him, I have to get over my past thoughts about him.

"See you around." He walks past me to the bank of offices along the wall.

"Yep." The word barely leaks out.

I don't think he heard my answer. Doesn't matter. We'll have plenty of time to get to know each other now that Dax and I aren't keeping our relationship a secret. Once we all start hanging out, I'm sure Tony won't be anything like his high school bully persona was.

Chapter Thirty-Four

-Rory-

Rain taps a happy dance against my kitchen window as I crack a third egg into the bowl of ground moose. I've decided to have a go at making Dax dinner tonight, not that I ever cook much. The chilly drizzle that's fallen all day has me in the mood for meatloaf, and my grandma's recipe's so easy, even I can't mess it up. I'm just hoping the ground-up pork rinds work as a carnivore substitute for the breadcrumbs.

P!nk blares through the speaker. I belt the lyrics in my off-key voice, a goofy smile on my face that hasn't left since this morning's workout. They say exercise gives you energy for the day, but I'd wager if they studied the benefits of exercise and being in love, the latter would win out. Hands down.

I push my fingers into the meat bowl. Cringing and trying not to gag, I mix it as quickly as I can and press it into a cake pan. The pan's my grandma's secret to meatloaf that didn't take forever to bake. It cuts the cook time in half, and you aren't left wondering if the middle's cooked all the way.

With my hands washed and the timer on, I grab my 1,000 Mile tea from Sipping Streams and sink into my couch. Raindrops splash onto the flowers just outside my window, making them bend and sway in a waltz. Rolling my eyes, I take a sip. Even a rainy day isn't dreary when one's hopped-up on love. I'll have to remember this feeling of expectant jubilation when I'm writing my next book.

My phone rings my friend Jodi's tone.

"You'll be very proud of me. The book's only two scenes away from being finished, *and* I think it might be the best one yet." I settle even further into the couch with my announcement.

"Good. That's good." That's not the response I was expecting, especially with how forced the enthusiasm sounds.

"What's wrong?" I push to the edge of my seat and set my mug on the coffee table. "Are you okay? Hurt?"

"I'm fine." She sighs long and loud, spreading goosebumps up my arms. "There's another video going viral."

My shoulders slump, but I push them back. It doesn't matter what some person looking for her fifteen minutes of bully fame thinks. In fact, if she wants to keep roasting me, I'll send her marshmallows.

"Don't care. She can be negative all she wants. I'll take the increase in sales from all her groupies grabbing my books to see just how bad they are." I reach for my tea.

"No, Rore. It's not her." Pity thickens Jodi's voice so much I could scoop it out and smear it on top of the meatloaf.

"It's not?" My phone dings in my ear.

She's sent me a text, but I don't think I want to open it.

"I'm so sorry, Rory." Her apology has my hand shaking as I put her on speaker and tap the text. "I've never seen a video go viral as fast as this one has. It's not even twelve hours old and already has over one and a half million views."

I hold my breath and tap the link. A video on Dax's personal account of him doing his impressive exercise where he hooks his legs around the end of the weight machine and holds himself parallel to the ground plays. My blood freezes as words pop onto the screen.

Ready for beast mode that will have ladies stumbling over themselves?

I watch myself hit the treadmill start button and go flying. More words scroll across.

Even if getting there causes pain …

I cringe as my foot on the screen connects with Dax's groin.

Romance author Bristol North fully approves of the results.

The video switches to me and Dax this morning doing pull ups, then changes to a different camera angle of us making out. It focuses in on Dax kissing along my neck, repeating the motion over and over again. I'm mortified by how the video has been edited to look like we're both shirtless.

Get Beast Mode. Get the Beauty.

It ends with a Bodies in Motion logo. The video loops back to the beginning, but I'm frozen. Dax's comment about bonehead moves and free publicity hit me like a tsunami.

How could he do this?

"I'm sorry, Rore. This is—" She cuts herself off with a sigh.

I tap the screen to close the app and stop the torture watching the video creates. It takes my trembling hands four times to get the mocking video off my screen. Doesn't help that everything blurs from tears.

"I've called in reinforcements. They should be there any minute."

Jodi did what? I try to ask, but my voice isn't working.

Car doors slam, dragging my gaze out the front window. Violet, Kemp, and Sadie rush up the driveway as Sadie's fiancé, Bjørn, pulls in behind Kemp's truck. I don't want them here, not when the embarrassment of my stupidity rips and tears at me.

But I can't move to the door to tell them to leave.

I can't breathe.

"Rory?" Jodi asks.

"Gotta go." Forcing the words out, I hang up on her.

I'm gulping air, but it's not doing any good. Sadie opens the door without even knocking, but I couldn't tell her to go away even if I wanted. My mouth moves, but nothing comes out.

How could I be so stupid?

How could I trust Dax after all he put me through in school?

Sadie and Violet's duplicate expressions of pity would be funny if I could feel anything past the sharp pain lacerating through me. I open my mouth to say I'm okay, but I choke on the lie.

"Rory, breathe." Sadie grabs my arms and shakes me.

It doesn't help. Nothing will. My eyes dart to my

phone, but all I see are shadows tunneling my vision to darkness.

Chapter Thirty-Five

-Dax-

I read the report on my computer for the fifth time and still don't know what it says. Most of today, I didn't have any issues with focus. Okay, sure, there may have been a time or two when I got caught up in thinking about Rory and zoned out, but, overall, I totally had my thoughts under control.

Until I got a text from Rory saying she's cooking dinner for me.

Now, my brain can't veer away from wondering if she's wearing an apron or dancing in her kitchen bare-footed while she cooks. It's probably archaic, but I can't get the picture out of my head. Honestly, all I want to do is be there with her, helping her putter around the kitchen—maybe plopping her on her kitchen counter and taking advantage of the cook time with some kissing.

I glance at my watch. Four-thirty's a good time to quit, especially since all I'm doing is wasting time. Reports can wait until tomorrow.

My phone vibrates on the desk. I glance at the caller ID and groan. I've zero interest in talking to Vince now. Tony passes in front of my office door, and guilt slumps my shoulders. If I want to move Bodies in Motion forward, I need to answer this call. It'll only take a few minutes, then I can head to Rory's.

"Vince, how's it going?" I put him on speaker and lean back in the chair.

"Great. Absolutely great."

There's more enthusiasm in his voice than I've ever heard. It's late on the East Coast. Maybe he's hit the bar a little too hard.

"Good to hear. You'll be pleased to hear that the program's going good. My client's results are beyond promising." I want to get right to the point and finish this call.

"Son, I couldn't care less about the program." His words slam into my gut like a sledgehammer.

"Sir?"

If I don't get this funding, how will we expand? I should have sent him updates, been better about measuring every improvement Rory saw.

"We'll be overnighting papers in the morning for you to sign."

My brain stalls its downward spiral.

"Wait. I'm confused." I hate to admit it, especially to this guy, but I'm having trouble keeping up. "If you aren't funding the program, why am I getting papers?"

"If I didn't fund you after that viral video, I might as well close up shop and retire."

What in the world's he talking about? My marketing department would have let me know if our posts were hitting. So far, they've been a waste of time and effort.

"That video and the thousand iterations popping up all over social media makes you worth your weight in gold, son. Men will pay insane amounts of money to be like you. And don't get me started about the women. To them, you're like an ice cream cone at fat camp, and every single one of them want a lick."

Ick.

My skin crawls with not only the insinuation but with dread. I've no clue what video he's talking about. If it has Vince foaming at the bit, it can't be good.

"Get the papers signed, then I want you down here by Friday," Vince demands, tightening my skin even more.

Like a straitjacket.

"Friday?" I need to get control of this conversation, but I'm floundering to even make sense of it.

"We have to capitalize on this exposure—keep the interest rolling. You'll be touring across the nation, flexing muscles and signing women's chests."

"Uhm, Vince—"

"Listen, I gotta run." He cuts me off, and now my anger kicks in. "Get that contract back to me by Thursday, son, and get ready to make millions."

Vince hangs up before I can respond. It irks, makes me want to wait until Saturday to sign, just to be contrary. But the irritation in his cockiness has nothing on the apprehension building in my gut. I slide through my apps on my phone until I find the never used social media ones and type in Bodies in Motion Gym.

The first one that shows up has large letters over the picture that read "Beast Mode" and has almost two million views. I tap on it and watch in horror as the video I thought I'd deleted plays on the screen. My hot anger incinerates the cold shock when I realize Rory's face is not only front and center, but her pen name's used to push the message. I tap out of the video to see how to take it down, but more posts fill the screen.

Posts on other people's accounts.

I scroll up, and they keep going.

There has to be hundreds of videos here.

And this is just one app. I swipe that app closed and open another. One quick search, and the video plays automatically at the top as the rest of the screen fills with more copies. The video switches from me taking one for the team to a completely different day. I'd been so focused on the words the first time, that I hadn't even noticed the change.

Tony.

He's the only one who saw us this morning and the only one who knew about the treadmill incident. My hand hurts from how hard I'm clenching it. I push from the desk with such force my chair crashes into the wall and tips over.

I storm out of the office. The instant people see me, they duck their heads or whisper to their friends. My gaze zeroes in on Tony at the front desk flirting with a client. It's a good thing the gym's full this afternoon. I'm so beyond enraged, I'm not sure what I'd do if Tony and I were alone.

As rage burns my chest with the need to make Tony pay, my pulse roars in my ears. I grind my teeth, needing to get control of my anger. I'm one wrong move away from snapping, just like I was that night I lost it with my dad.

That thought pulls me up short, making a tremor surge through my body. I won't pummel Tony, even though he deserves it. I can't, not if I don't want to be like my dad.

The woman who Tony's flirting with sees me coming. Her eyes widen, and she quickly says goodbye and leaves. I step up right next to Tony.

"Take. It. Down," I growl through gritted teeth so I don't yell.

"Can't, man. It's got a life of its own now." Tony shrugs and tips his chin to the packed workout area. "Good thing too. We've doubled our membership, and that's just here."

"I don't care about a bunch of ambulance chasers. I told you not to post the video." I take a deep breath to calm myself.

His lack of regret isn't making it easy on me.

"You should be thanking me." Tony turns to me with fire in his eyes and a tight smile. "That thirty-second video's going to make us millions, and you know it. I can't believe you've gone so soft."

"I don't want *my* company humiliating someone to get ahead."

"Please. That video's going to do just as much business for Scaredy as it will for us. People will be scrambling to read her smut now that they think you're her inspiration."

My fist connects to his nose with a loud crack. Blood spurts across the tile floor and down my shirt as Tony stumbles backward. The room stills in an unnatural silence.

"Pack your stuff and get out of my gym." I step close and grab the front of his shirt. "If you ever hurt Rory again, I'll break more than your nose."

I push him away from me and rush toward the door,

pointing at two of my guys on my way out. "Escort him out, and make sure he doesn't take anything."

Tony cusses behind me, but I just ignore him. I need to get to Rory and explain. It's a good thing none of the cops catch my frantic race through town. With her dad being the chief of police, I'd probably end up in jail instead of just slapped with a ticket, especially if he thinks I had anything to do with the video.

Rory's house comes into view and my heart drops at all the vehicles parked there. I don't want an audience, not now. I want the freedom to hold her and beg her to forgive me. I swerve to the curb and slam the truck into park.

When I get to the front door, Kemp and one of the guys from his party come out to meet me.

"Seriously, dude?" Kemp crosses his arms, spearing me with a look of extreme disappointment.

"It wasn't me." I hold up my hands, praying that they'll let me by without having to muscle my way in.

The guy who has ex-military written all over him scoffs. I glare at him. He might be able to kill me a hundred ways, but I'm at least half a foot taller. I won't go down easy.

"You need to leave." Kemp drops his hands.

"I *need* to see Rory, to explain." I lean to look through the window, but I can't see through the sheer curtains.

"She doesn't want to see you. Not now." Kemp crosses his arms again.

"I didn't do this," I yell as my frustration and anger push past my restraint.

I step forward, but Kemp puts his hand on my chest.

He looks over his shoulder at the door, sighs, and turns back to me. He shakes his head, his expression wary.

"I hope that's the case, but she doesn't want you here right now." He clenches his jaw and lifts an eyebrow. "And you have to respect what she wants."

I swallow my desperation as I drag my gaze from the door to Kemp and back. I nod and step away. The cold drizzle drenching me chills me all the way to my core. No matter how much I want to, I can't force Rory to see me.

I take another step back, then turn and stomp away. My instincts scream to stay, to make her see the truth. But the thought of doing that seems too much like my dad forcing my mom not to leave and pushes acid up my throat.

I stare at the house for a long moment before I throw the truck in drive. I won't make her talk to me. But I'll do everything I can to make this right.

Chapter Thirty-Six

-Rory-

I stare into the empty fireplace, wishing there were flames flickering there. I've been cold—hollow—since that video ruined everything. I'm too empty to even take the time to build a fire.

My head lays on Emmy's lap, and her fingers run through my hair. She arrived last night, left work without explaining, and I'm so glad she did. Her being here's the only thing that's brought me comfort.

"I hope Brad doesn't fire you for just dropping everything and coming down." I close my eyes to her soothing touch.

I'm surprised she's been able to be so calm. Usually, the amount of nothingness we've done today would drive her loco.

She scoffs. "Please. That man would be lost without me."

"Oh, really?" I flop onto my back and look up at her.

"Why's your eyebrow raised like that?" Emmy

pushes her finger onto my forehead. "There's nothing between Brad and me except annoyance. I drive him wild with my lack of order, and his lists and obsessions make me insane. Even if there was something there, we are so completely opposite that it would never work."

"So, you're telling me you aren't attracted to your insanely hot boss who happens to be worth millions and has a passion for all things extreme outdoors like you do?"

There's a hesitation in her nod. "Yep."

"I knew it!" I wag my pointers up at her like guns.

She shoves me from her lap. I tumble off the couch and barely catch myself before I crush Chub. He doesn't even notice his life just rush past his eyelids. I peck him on the forehead, then hop onto the couch.

"You can't hide from me." I push her shoulder.

She stares at me, denial in her eyes. Then something shifts, like an idea clicked in her head, and the gleam in her eyes has me more than a little nervous. My throat goes dry, and I scoot to the opposite side of the couch and pull my knees to my chest.

"Okay. You're totally right." She settles against the couch arm so she's facing me. "Brad's tempting. Like Grandma's homemade marshmallows over a campfire. Remember those?"

"Oh my gosh." I close my eyes and moan at the memory of their gooey sweetness. "So. Stinking. Good."

"Right."

"But how does Brad remind you of marshmallows?"

"Because, just like those little fluffy bites of heaven, if I just give one inch in to letting myself consider more with him than what we have right now, I'll become obsessed." She smiles sadly and shrugs. "He's that good.

That addicting. I can't risk it when we're so completely wrong for each other."

"Em." I hug my knees tighter.

"Plus, I have the coolest job ever. I'm not about to lose getting paid to play and have fun for a very, very, *very* slim chance he might be interested too." She shudders. "Imagine me in an office, like actually behind a desk and everything. No way. Not worth it."

"There are other jobs that are outdoors, you know."

"Yeah, but they're *jobs*." She says the last word like it tastes nasty. "What I do now isn't. Not even close."

I nod and put my chin on my knees. "I get that."

She crosses her legs, and I can see it coming. "When are you going to talk to Dax?"

I shake my head. "I can't. Not after that. I'm completely mortified." My face heats thinking about how I'd practically climbed up Dax like a horny koala bear, and my family saw it. "Dad threatened to find a shallow hole in the mountains. I guess there's one he knows right next to a bear's den Dax would fit perfect in."

"Yeah, but Kemp said Dax didn't post it."

"How can we know that? Bully, remember? He even told me using videos like that's common practice to gain publicity." But even as I say that, I know it's not true.

Dax would never hurt someone intentionally, especially just to get ahead. With the way Emmy rolls her eyes, she doesn't believe me either. I take a deep breath into my too tight lungs and say the words that have been circling in my head all night and day.

"I just want to go back to being safe—to being anonymous, a nobody. Being invisible's a lot less painful." I bite my lip and twist my fingers into my sweats. "I should've just started dating Mark when he asked me. I mean, I'd never be publicly humiliated with him."

"You wouldn't have sizzling sparks, either. More like plain white rice."

"You don't know that."

"Please. Don't fool yourself." Emmy leans forward. "I watched that video, several times actually. You and Dax are so completely in love it's both sickening and toe curling at the same time. I mean, the way he helped you with those pull ups was like total swoon. Then the look on his face when you kissed him—" She fans herself. "If there was a snowbank, I'd be jumping in it."

I cover my face with my hands and groan. "Yeah, but I don't want the entire world to see that. At least with Mark, any looks that happen stay between us."

"Rore—"

"I would probably grow to love Mark like he loves me," I insist, though a rock settles in my gut.

"Neither of you deserve that. Not Mark. Nor you." She places her hand on my knee, getting way more serious than Emmy normally does. "Don't you want passion—tingles? Isn't that worth a little embarrassment or discomfort? Or are all your books purely fantasy and happily ever after's actually just a fairytale?"

Her words jab straight into my heart. I press my hand to my chest. "That's not fair."

"The truth isn't always."

I growl and glare at her. "I hate you."

"I know." She looks toward the door. "And you're about to hate me even more."

Has Dax come back? The fact that he hasn't—hasn't called past the one time he begged to talk—keeps disappointment threading through my already confused mind. I whip my head around, my shoulders slumping at Mark walking up to the door.

"Remember what I just said." She goes to the door. "Sizzle and passion or white rice." She grabs her purse and opens the door before Mark can knock. "Hey, Mark. Perfect timing. I was just heading to the store for rice."

"See ya, Em." He steps in, his gaze focusing on me and not leaving. "You okay?"

I shrug. Behind his back, Emmy mouths 'sizzle' and even puts up jazz fingers before abandoning me. My heart bangs against my chest. What do I even say to him?

"I'm really sorry." He sits in Emmy's spot on the opposite side of the couch.

We haven't talked since he stormed out of the kennel two weeks ago. It's the longest we've ever gone without contacting each other. I've hated it, but I also couldn't bring myself to reach out, not with my relationship with Dax getting more serious. Mark made it clear he didn't want to be around me if I was with Dax.

"Why are you apologizing?"

"Because I don't like to see you hurt." Mark swallows. "Even if it means I might now have a chance."

The pounding of my heart's now in my throat. What if I give him a chance and see if I could love him more than just a friend?

Would that be so bad?

I scan his face. Sure, he's handsome. He's a sweet guy with a big heart. But the thought of kissing him turns my stomach, like I'd be kissing my brother, if I had one.

But if I say no to him, will the only friendship I've had outside my family since childhood end?

"Do you really love me that way, or is it just because we're comfortable with each other?" I ask before I can talk myself out of it.

"What do you mean? Of course, I love you." Mark's eyebrows scrunch together.

"But how do you feel when I'm with you?"

"I feel warmth. Ease." He shakes his head like he's trying to find the right answer. "You're my constant."

"But no sizzle," I whisper.

"There's more than sizzle, Rore. At least for me, there's so much dang heat it constantly boils." He clenches his jaw and stares into the empty fireplace. "Have you ever watched a kid with a sparkler? How it pops and flashes bright, but quickly dies out."

"Yeah," I choke out.

"Is that what you really want? A momentary jolt of excitement that leaves you in the dark, or do you want something that's more lasting? More steady?"

"Both." My nose tingles, and I sniff.

He turns sad eyes on me. "You can't have both. They don't exist together."

My heart drops, leaving me shaking. I push my fingers through my hair and press my eyes closed to the tears forming.

Maybe he's right.

Maybe having both is just fiction.

But what if he's wrong? I trail my finger down my ear and along the word there. I can't feel the letters, but their meaning sears me. Taunts me to ignite my dreams, even if I come away burned.

Chapter Thirty-Seven

-Dax-

Rushing around the hood of my truck, I open the passenger door and help Mom out. When she smiles at me, it's one of pure love like she used to give before the injury. No confusion or asking who I am. Her brain has improved so much on the high-fat, zero-carb diet that her neurologist has been calling me to get my research sources.

Her presence is exactly what I need right now, even if she didn't remember me. Rory hasn't called me back yet. I've picked up my phone a thousand times to text or call her again. Had my keys in my hand twice that many times. But I'm not going to force her to talk to me—to see me—when it's clear she doesn't want to.

Mom wraps her hand through my arm, so I lead her up to my house. I've been so busy with working on the expansion and spending time with Rory that I haven't brought Mom over to tend the flowers. I'll be even more absent if I sign the papers that arrived yesterday.

It's everything I wanted, all the money we'd need to

grow big. Two months ago, I'd have the ink drying before the UPS carrier would be out the door. I've been trying to nail down just what's holding me back. It's more than just my messed-up brain over Rory.

It's like I don't know what I want anymore.

And that scares me.

"Oh, Dax," Mom says. "Look at all the weeds you've let in."

I try my best to push my spinning thoughts about Rory and Vince's proposal to the back of my mind and focus on Mom.

"I told you I desperately needed you." I open the front door and motion for her to go in.

"You haven't needed me a day in your life." She pats me on the chest. "Always so full of life."

My throat closes with emotion that I try to swallow down. "You're wrong, Mom. I have always needed you."

And now it's like I finally got her back.

She beams at me, then turns her attention to the pictures. Her fingers drag along the top of the frame with me and her in it. In the past, she'd look at that picture and talk like I was still a child. With her brain damage, I was a little boy "off to camp," no matter the season. I stopped trying to explain that I wasn't her little boy anymore.

I tense.

Will she regress to her confusion being here?

She sighs. "This was the best summer. Do you remember?"

I stare at her, amazed that she's pulling up memories we assumed were long gone and holding my breath for the moment she forgets again. "I remember being happy."

That hadn't happened often.

In fact, that's about the only time I remember being so.

"Your grandma stayed with us that summer." Mom picks up the photo of Memaw. "Your father didn't dare touch us when she was around."

I whip my gaze up from the photo to Mom. She never talks about the abuse. Her forehead furrows and shoulders droop in sadness.

"She begged me to take you and go live with her."

"She knew?"

Mom shakes her head. "She suspected."

"Why didn't you?"

"Stupidity." She shrugs. "Those months, your father gave me a glimpse of who I'd fallen in love with in high school, and I stubbornly thought he'd realized he didn't need to hit us anymore. We were happy. *He* was happy." She scoffs. "It only took two days after Memaw left for him to get right back at knocking us around."

"Why not leave then? Why stay?" I don't understand how she could've had an out for us all those years, but she kept us trapped.

"He said he'd kill her and drag us back here if we ever left." Mom turns glassy eyes on me. "And I believed him." Her chin trembles. "I'm so sorry, Dax. I was a coward and put you through so much pain."

I pull her into my arms. "*He* did, Mom. Not you. And I could've stopped him sooner than I did."

She's shaking her head against my chest.

"Yeah, I could have. I was stronger than him since my sophomore year, but I was afraid too." I hug her, wrapping my body around hers. "But we don't have to worry about him anymore. He'll never hurt us again. We get to move on, to have a happy life full of friends."

"And flowers." She peeks up at me.

I smile down at her. "Lots of flowers."

"I don't deserve you."

"I'm blessed to have you as my mom and wouldn't want it any other way."

She sniffs, and I kiss her on the forehead.

"Look at us carrying on when there's work to do." She pats my chest. "Go get the gardening tools, and I'll meet you out back."

I step toward the garage, lighter somehow. Grabbing the tool caddy, I huff out all the lingering resentment I've held onto for too long. The best thing I can do for revenge is have a life so full of happiness that it blasts the darkness of my past away. To be the opposite of him in every way.

I set the caddy down and kneel in the grass beside Mom. She carefully digs the trowel into the soft, rich soil and pulls an offending weed from between the flowers. If I'm gone all the time expanding my business, will she forget me again? While she's better, she's not healed all the way. There's no way I can drag her around with me. Routine and familiarity keeps her mind stronger.

"How's it going with Rory? Will I see her today? She said she'd love to help me with the flowers." Mom tosses a weed into a pile. "She's so lovely. I think you've found a keeper there."

I was hoping to keep the focus away from what's bothering me, but I should've known that Rory would win Mom over with just one meeting.

"It's not going well at all." I yank out a weed with a

bit too much force and pull up a baby poppy with it. "I don't think you'll be seeing her anymore."

"What happened?" Mom sits back, leans to one side, and motions with her hand for me to talk. "Spill it. Don't keep anything from me."

So, I do. I tell her everything. How I bullied Rory in school so her dad wouldn't take me to foster care even though I'm pretty sure I loved her way back then. How we made a deal that turned into so much more. I tell my mom about the gym's expansion and Vince's offer. She gets riled when I tell about Tony's video and forces me to show it to her.

"Oh, my." Her eyes widen and cheeks pink. "I can see why that would go viral."

My neck heats.

"That boy has been nothing but trouble since first grade." She tugs on a weed and holds it up. "You have to pull those toxic people out of your life, Dax. We spent too much time in vileness to allow it anymore."

"I know." I brush my fingertip along a poppy petal. "I'm done with him."

"This Vince fellow sounds like a pea in Tony's pod."

My lips tweak in amusement. "Yeah. He kind of is."

"Then why in the world would you go into cahoots with him?" Mom's roommates are rubbing off on her.

"I can't go nationwide without funding."

"And why exactly do you want to do that?"

"I don't know. So we don't lack like we always did."

She throws her arms wide. "Does it look like we're lacking?"

I glance around the massive yard and too-big house. I don't need all of this, not for just me.

"Dax, what makes you happy? Really happy?" Mom places her hand on my knee.

I want to spew the first thought that pops in my head, something lame like helping people. That's just a platitude without real meaning. So, I close my eyes and really think about my answer.

When am I happiest?

Surprisingly, it's not at the gym. I enjoy it, yes. I love the challenge on myself, both mentally and physically; love seeing others push hard. But there's a weight that's always on me there.

My happiest is when I'm on the pitch with the kids. Seeing their excitement, watching them grow into young men and women of strength and honor, that's when I'm happiest.

I picture Rory in the stands in Anchorage, cheering like a wild woman for the team. I feel her fingers running through my hair in the ambulance. Hear her whisper-soft words of comfort as she kisses me. She's beyond happiness.

She's home.

Life.

If I don't have her with me, then what's the point?

"Rugby and Rory." I open my eyes and stare at my mom. "That's what makes me happy."

"Can you have those with the business you have now?"

"Yes."

"What about when you expand?" Mom lifts an eyebrow, fully knowing the answer.

"No." I shake my head. "Not if I'm gone all the time."

"Then there's your answer." She sits back like everything in the world's right again. "You're already a rich man, Dax Payton. Why sacrifice your happiness when you don't have to?"

"It might be too late." I pluck a petal from a flower.

"Have you tried?"

"No."

"Well, why the devil not?" She shoves my shoulder.

"I don't want to force Rory." I shake my head. "I can't be like Dad."

"You have never been and will never be like that man." Mom stabs the trowel into the dirt. "It's not like you're going to drag her into your house and not let her go. You woo her, and she'll forgive you. Besides, it wasn't you who posted that video, and from what I saw on it, that Rory's wild about you, Dax."

"Well, I'm wild about her too."

"So let's come up with a plan." Mom claps her hands in excitement.

I run the petal between my fingers as a smile blooms across my face. "I think I have an idea."

Chapter Thirty-Eight

I rub my slick hands on the eighth pair of pants I've tried on and step out of the closet. Emmy sits up fast from where she lays on my bed. Her eyes go wide, and her mouth drops before she does a gig and scrambles off the bed.

"Oh my gosh, Rore. You look stunning. This one's definitely it." She steps around me, fingering the off-shoulder, sheer sleeve of the tunic.

"You sure?" I look in the mirror, wanting to throw up.

The skinny jeans make my legs look a mile long. I've never actually been brave enough to wear the sheer tunic over a spaghetti tank top, even though I fell in love with it at the store. I just never felt I pulled off the sexy look. I turn, checking out my backside.

"Absolutely. You look like Sandy at the end of *Grease,* only better, since you've had the outfit for years and didn't change just for some man." Emmy shakes her head. "I never did understand that. I mean, I guess he changed for her, too, but why was she the only one who stayed changed? Like, sure, Danny was way sexier as the bad boy, but—"

"Emmy. Focus." I motion my hand up and down myself. "Am I ready? Do I need to do anything more?"

"Are you kidding?" She jumps from foot to foot and gives me a hug. "You're gorgeous. This outfit's killer, and, if you change one more time, you're just stalling. Wildes. Don't. Stall."

I lean my head to the side and cringe. I'm pretty good at delaying anything and everything that's uncomfortable. What I'm about to do is so far from my zone it might as well be Pluto. Emmy lifts an eyebrow and spears me with a look that would stop a charging bear.

"Fine. Wildes don't stall." I hold up my hands in surrender. "Okay. Let's do this before I lose my nerve and curl up in the pile of clothes, mumbling incoherently."

She grabs my phone, opens the app she loaded earlier that connects all the social medias, and raises the camera to point at me. "Ready to go live?"

"No." There's seriously so much sweat on my palms, wiping them does nothing.

Emmy lowers the phone. "You don't have to do this. If you changed into sweats and one of your book shirts, washed the makeup off, and headed to the privacy of his house, he'd still swoop you into his arms the instant he saw you."

"You don't know that."

"I've got great intuition, and I've obsessed over that video." She's not the only one.

After the twentieth time, I stopped being mortified and saw what I couldn't see before. Dax Payton might just love me as much as I love him. The only reason I'm doubting is because he hasn't tried to explain past the one voicemail.

I shake my hands, letting the doubt fling off. "No. A grand gesture isn't grand unless it's epic. Plus, this has just as much to do with me getting over my social media fear as it does getting my man back."

"All righty, then." She lifts the phone up. "You're live in three, two, one."

She points at me, and I huff out a breath. The smile I give the camera wobbles, but I can't help that.

"Hey, everyone. I'm romance author Bristol North. You may know me from the viral bad book review of *Washed Up*, or maybe more recently from the gym fail at Bodies In Motion." I lift my hands and turn from side to side. "As you can see, I've recovered from the tread-mill incident, but you probably already noticed that from the second half of the video that's making its rounds."

I wink at whoever's watching. Wink! I chuckle and duck my head at my boldness as heat travels up my chest.

"Bristol, hearts and laughing emojis are flying on the screen." Emmy's use of my pen name confuses me for a second. "You've got lots of people here watching."

"Well, then, I guess I better talk." I clear my throat when my voice wobbles and focus on the phone's round camera. "I usually run away from social media like it's a pack of starved wolves. I'm definitely more an injured caribou at the back of the herd type of person rather than the alpha leading the pack. So, why am I dressed up and talking to you?"

"Questions are popping up on the screen faster than

I can read them," Emmy says. "Aah, and they all say you're beautiful."

"Do you think I'll have Dax drooling?" I ask the viewers.

"ReadEmAndWeep says you'll have him on his knees, bowing in worship."

The screen name twists in my stomach. She's the one that started all this with her nasty review. I could easily give her a taste of her own medicine. Yet, all my anger over her review and videos doesn't burn anymore.

"Oh, ReadEm, I don't want him on his knees. I want him. Period. And since this all started with you, I'm glad you're here so I can say 'thank you.'" I tip my head toward the bedroom door. "But we won't find the love of my life here, so I'm hoping y'all will come with me to search him out."

"They're game." Emmy giggles. "More than game."

"Okay."

I head out of the room, surprised at how much fun I'm actually having despite my knees threatening to buckle beneath me. I thought for sure I'd be stumbling over my words, possibly vomiting in front of the world. I walk backward toward the front door so I can talk to the camera.

"So, a little update. I may have freaked out a bit about the whole viral treadmill video." I cringe.

"A bit?" Emmy quips.

"Hey. No lip from the camerawoman." I point my finger at her, then focus on the phone. "She's right, though. I haven't talked to Dax since the day it posted. I was afraid and hurt. I'm not sure if any of you can relate, but I was—am—pretty shy, and having something so humiliating happen, then having all the world see it, was like high school gym class on steroids."

Emmy gives a thumbs up. "Lots of people get that."

"While Dax didn't have anything to do with the video being posted, he was my nemesis growing up." I bite my lip. "Enemies to lovers has always been one of my favorite tropes. It's even more so now." I wag my eyebrows. "Anyhoo, I let my past overshadow my future and turned him away when he came to explain. Hopefully, he won't reciprocate."

I pause with my hand on the front doorknob and stare at the floor. I really, really hope that's not the case. Taking a deep breath, I look at the camera and shrug.

"I guess we'll find that out together." My smile trembles, and Emmy gives me a nod of encouragement. "Okay. We're off to find Dax and make him weak in the knees."

I swing the door open and rush out before I lose my courage. My feet trip, and I pull up short. Bright yellow poppies and purply blue irises in hodgepodge containers fill my walkway and yard.

Dax bends over one that keeps tipping over in the middle of the yard while his mom tells him he's doing it all wrong. The mason jar falls over, and Dax growls, pulling his hands through his hair and making it stick straight up.

Emmy pushes me from behind, and I stumble forward. Dax's mom sees me at the same time and taps her fingers on the side of his head. He throws his hands out.

"I know, Mom. I'm trying." He grabs the jar and twists it on the ground.

"No, Dax. Look." She pushes him again.

He finally sees me and slowly stands. There's so much vulnerability in the droop of his shoulders and the sad downturn of his eyes. I blink to clear my vision, but it doesn't help.

He's come.

Made a grand gesture of his own.

I dart my eyes at what must be every single flower from his yard and his mom's. Tears stream down my face unchecked.

"Don't just stand there," Emmy says, jolting me from my shock.

I take off for him, hurdling flowers as best as I can. He meets me halfway, and I throw myself at him. I have no doubt he'll catch me.

"I'm sorry, Rory." He buries his face into my neck as I wrap my legs around his waist. "I'm so sorry."

I shake my head. "It wasn't you."

"But—" His arms tighten around me. "How do you know that?"

"Dax, that's not who you are." I pull back enough to look in his eyes. "I'm just sorry I pushed you away like I did, jumping to the worst conclusion. I'm trying to be better about not going into self-protection, turtle mode, but I failed. Deep down, though, I know you'd never hurt me intentionally. And you'd definitely never humili- iate me."

"Never." His whisper's hoarse and forceful as he leans his forehead on mine.

"I love you, Dax Payton, and I want my adventures in life to be shared with you."

"I've been in love with you since the third grade, Aurora Wilde." Dax trails his finger along my ear tattoo. "I'm finally ready to be brave and let that love ignite."

I spear my fingers through his hair and kiss him. This is no sizzling kiss. It's an explosion of heat, love, and hopefulness within me. I can't help smiling as I turn my head to get a better angle.

A giggle hits my ears, then his mom says, "That will get the neighbor riled."

Like that's a good thing.

My face burns hot as I hide it in Dax's neck.

"Um … why's your cousin recording us?" His voice rumbles against my ear.

"Oh." I unwrap my legs.

He puts me down but holds me tight to him. I peck his cheek before turning to the camera. I can't believe I forgot this was on video. My face heats even more as I motion to Emmy.

"Welp, world, looks like he takes me back."

His wide eyes that were staring at the phone snap to me. "You never lost me. Never will."

My cheeks hurt so bad from the smile on my face. He bends down, his lips lingering right below my ear.

"Remember, Cupcake, I'm wild about you, completely addicted." He kisses my neck, and my knees go all wobbly. "There's no way I'm letting you go now."

I look at the phone and stifle a nervous giggle. "Go find yourself an adventure." I gaze up at Dax. "The gym's a good place to start."

Awe and love wash over me as he smiles down at me. This man, my supposed enemy, is everything I've longed for. He's my book boyfriend come to life, but so much better than I could ever imagine. I can't wait to see what the next chapter holds.

Chapter Thirty-Nine

-Dax-

Crossing my arms to keep me from dashing down the sideline, I watch as Skye breaks from the ruck toward the touchline. Being a coach is brutal. All I want to do is join in the game. I glance over at the scoreboard. We're only two points ahead in the championship game with just under two minutes to go.

This match has been one of the most intense matches I've ever been a part of. That's what you hope for in a championship, but this one's almost too close. Two giant bruisers barrel toward Skye, and I clench my teeth together to keep from yelling across the field. The team knows what to do.

Skye glances to her side. The team captain, James, hollers something at her. The forwards are almost on her, so she moves to toss the ball sideways to James.

Halfway through the motion, she performs a dummy, spinning away from James and tucking the ball against her body. I'm not sure where she learned that move, but its poetic. For a second, the two forwards fall for it, turning their attack toward James. By the time they realize they've been duped, Skye's fifteen feet away and sprinting for the try line.

I peek up at the stands. Rory and my mom jump up and down, clutching each other and cheering for Skye. Rory bought face paint in the team's colors, and she and Mom look like female versions of Mel Gibson and the Scots in *Braveheart.*

It's been a crazy month since our viral video. When I turned down Vince's money, Clay, the only member of the investor group I actually liked, called and offered to fund me himself. Saying no to him was a lot harder, but after a lot of prayer and talking to Rory and Mom, going nationwide really isn't what I want.

This is.

Being on the pitch with rugby's future.

Having the love of my life cheering us on with war paint smeared across her face.

Nothing could ever compare to this.

Mom and Rory hug each other, and the warmth of rightness spreads through my chest. I pull my gaze from them to the in-goal where the team surrounds Skye in a massive group hug. We've just won the match.

James calls the kicker in for an attempt. James will make a good leader when he grows up. I'm looking forward to being here for that. The opposing team charges, and the kick goes wide.

The ref whistle blows the end of the game, and the team goes wild. Fans and parents flood the field. In the mayhem, I lose sight of Rory and Mom. Parents shake my hand and clap me on the shoulder as they join the celebration. Each "Thanks for being here for my boy, Coach," or "Rugby has changed my kid," fills me with even more confirmation that turning down the money was the right decision.

"Dax!" Rory yells behind me.

I turn just in time to catch her as she launches herself at me. Funny how she likes to cling to me like she's a koala and I'm a eucalyptus tree. Not that I'm complaining.

"We won!" She lifts her arms over her head.

She's been to every single practice. When she arrives with Chub under one arm and snacks under the other, the team always rushes to help. Every question she asks, they answer her in detail. I kind of think they're all hoping she'll write a rugby romance series or something. So, her saying "we" seems like the most natural word.

"Yep. We did." And not just the championship.

Her grin's huge on her blue face. I run one hand up her back to pull her in for a kiss. She wraps her arms around me, not needing much encouragement.

Just before our lips touch, her eyes go wide. Frigid, sickly-sweet orange crashes over us. She spurts and scrambles from my arms. I turn to find two of our forwards holding the drink cooler and the rest of the team cheering around them.

The team rushes me, surrounding me in a sort of chaotic ruck. We bounce as one as we chant our victory song. When my gaze snags Rory's, she's hugging Mom as they watch the celebration. My life has been far from easy, but this moment right here couldn't be more perfect.

Emmy's story will be releasing next. To get updates on when her story is available, a free Alaskan Rebel novelette, and other specials, sign up for Sara's newsletter.

For more Alaskan adventures and Wilde family antics, read A Rebel's Beacon.

Wild Hearts of Alaska

Wild about Denali

Wild about Violet

Wild about Rory

<u>Other Books</u>

Meeting Up with the Consultant

About the Author

Sara Blackard is an award-winning romance novelist who writes stories that thrill the imagination and strum heartstrings. When she's not crafting wild adventures and romances that make readers swoon, she's home-schooling her four adventurous boys and one fearless princess, keeping their off-grid house running (don't ask if it's clean), or enjoying the Alaskan lifestyle she and her Hunky Hubster love. Visit her website at www.sarablackard.com